Gemini Killer

A Mark Peterson Novel

D M Gaines

The Gemini Killer

ISBN 978-0-6158753-3-0
Library of Congress Control Number: 201394503

Editing and cover design by
Tiffany Rucker
tiffanyrucker@yahoo.com
Revised August 2013

www.newflavorbooksandpublishingllc.com
New Flavor Books is an imprint of New Flavor Books
& Publishing LLC

New Flavor Books & Publishing LLC
PO Box 603376 Cleveland, Ohio 44105

Acknowledgments

First I would like to thank God for blessing me with the gift to write. He showed me that each one of us possess a special gift within us. Next I would like to thank Poetic Gangster, every book that I write I have to thank him for helping me hone a skill that I did not even know I had.

I would like to thank the Florida boys Pep and Twin, for being my proofreaders. If they gave their approval then I knew the book was a go. Last, I would like to thank all of you, the fans. I hope that you see my versatility and like the fact that I'm not scared to go outside the box. Thanks for your support.

Sincerely D.M Gaines

Mary Weathers worked as a nurse at the Metropolitan hospital in Cleveland, Ohio. Most people that came in contact with Mary thought that she should have been a model instead of a nurse. She stood 5' 2", had a slim, athletic looking body and the face of an angel. She had hypnotic emerald green eyes.

Because Mary had the face of a model and the body of an Olympic gymnast, while at work she got hit on by everyone. Doctors, nurses and even patients hit on Mary.

Mary did not mind the attention that men gave her at work, but there was only one man that she was interested in. She was head over heels for her boyfriend of over two years, Cody Miller.

She and Cody had been living together for over a year and she could not wait to get off of work so that she could go home and climb into bed with him.

Mary was sitting at her work station waiting for 11:30pm to come so that she could make her last rounds. She worked a twelve hour shift, from twelve in the afternoon until twelve midnight. She looked at the clock again for the third time and found that she had fifteen minutes left before it would be time for her to make her last rounds.

Sitting at her station, she started thinking about Cody and she found that thinking about him brought wetness in between her thighs.

Mary had a high sex drive and she regretted that her and Cody worked different shifts. The both of them working different shifts prevented Mary from getting sex as much as she wanted.

She knew that Cody was probably at home in bed, sleeping peacefully. Sitting there, she felt the urge to have sex and she made up her mind that when she got home she was going to climb under the sheets and give Cody some oral sex. She knew that even if he was in a deep sleep, some good oral sex would awaken him. She also knew that once Cody's penis came to life and he woke up that he would want to have a full sex session.

Mary smiled as she pictured them having wild and passionate sex. She snapped out of her thoughts, looked back up at the clock and seen that she was ten minutes late on making her rounds. She jumped up grabbed her clipboard and headed to make her rounds.

James and Jerry were sitting in a car that was parked inside of Metro Hospital's parking garage. Jerry was waiting on an unsuspecting victim to arrive in the garage. He was about to kidnap a person that he intended to make one of his patients. He forced James to come with him to be a witness to the kidnapping.

Jerry and James were once best friends, but as of late it seemed to him that James had been trying to distance himself from him and his murderous ways.

Jerry felt that when he used his wicked, murderous ways to relieve James from the life of torture he had been living in as a kid, him being a killer did not bother James.

Jerry sat there, thinking that if it wasn't for him, James would not be in the position that he was in. Because of the favor he had done for James, he felt that James would forever owe him.

He looked over at James sitting in the passenger's seat looking nervous and scared out of his wits. He could see James' body trembling and sweat dripping from his forehead.

To see James in that condition was pleasing to Jerry. He enjoyed seeing James squirm and feeling uncomfortable.

Jerry despised the fact that since James had become a doctor he started acting like he was better than Jerry and too good to participate in the kidnappings and murders that he was doing.

Jerry also resented the fact that James would not acknowledge him as being a doctor also. Even without a paper stating that, Jerry considered himself a doctor. He considered himself to be the doctor of death and he considered the setup that he had in the basement of their home to be the location of his private practice.

The more he sat there thinking about the changes that had taken place between him and James the angrier he became.

His Isotoner gloved hands, tightly gripped the steering wheel as he thought about how James had snubbed his nose at him when he asked him to help him kidnap the woman from his job.

When he had asked James to participate his response was, "You're crazy!" He calling Jerry crazy had set something off inside of him.

Jerry had gotten an overwhelming urge to kill James, but he realized that killing James would be too easy. He decided that he would make James suffer emotionally and mentally. He brought up the secret that he and James shared to force him to participate in the kidnapping.

Coming out of his deep thoughts, Jerry looked at his watch, then turned to James and said, "It's time."

Jerry took the keys out of the ignition, got out of the car and headed back to the trunk. He put the key into the trunk, opened it then leaned over into the trunk as if he was looking for something.

λ

Mary was in the hospital's elevator. She had finally gotten off of work and couldn't wait to get home to Cody.

She intended to follow through with her plan in hopes that Cody would wake up and give her some good, fulfilling sex.

She stepped off the elevator onto the third level of the hospital's parking garage. Soon as she exited the elevator, she took her keychain out of her purse. She did that for two reasons, one was to use the car remote to unlock her car door the other reason was to have access to the can of mace that was on her keychain. Even though the parking garage had a security guard down on the first level, Mary still felt nervous walking through the darkened parking garage late at night.

Cody had tried to persuade her to purchase a licensed firearm for her protection but Mary had refused. She was scared that if she were ever forced to use it that she might end up hurting herself or an innocent bystander.

She reached the last row, where her car was parked, when she turned down the row, she noticed a man bent over inside of a trunk of a car that was parked next to hers. She stopped in her tracks and grabbed a hold of her mace.

All of a sudden the man rose up out of the trunk of the car holding a crowbar in his hand. He turned in Mary's direction and relief came over her. She recognized him as being someone she seen at the hospital frequently.

She did not know his job title, but she knew that she seen him in the hospital a lot. Feeling relieved she started walking towards her car and when she got to it, she said to him, "It looks like you have a problem?"

"Unfortunately yes, I have a flat tire and I do not have my triple A card on me. I was intending to change it myself, but it seems that I do not have all of the required tools."

"What exactly do you need?"

"Well I have this," he said showing her the crowbar. "But, I do not have a jack to go with it," he continued.

"I think I may have one, let me check." She used the remote to open her trunk. She bent over inside of it and got to moving things out of the way so that she could get to the compartment that held the jack.

She got to the compartment, opened it and grabbed the jack, "Yes I have one," she said as she pulled the jack out of the compartment.

She was about to rise out of the trunk, when Jerry raised the crowbar and brought it down in a swinging motion, hitting her on the base of her skull. Mary's body went limp and she slumped inside of the trunk, while at the same time dropping her purse to the ground.

Jerry lifted Mary out of the trunk and dragged her over to James' trunk. He placed her into the trunk, shut it, then hurried back over to her car and closed her trunk.

Afterwards, he calmly walked back over to James' car and got in.

While putting the key into the ignition, he looked over at James with a smile on his face. The expression that was on James' face, caused him to replace his smile with a look of disgust on his face.

He started the car and pulled out of the parking space. To him, James looked pathetic sitting there. Jerry was tired of James acting like a coward and he decided that he was going to keep forcing James to be involved in his madness until he started showing some guts.

Jerry, drove the car at a fast pace until he reached the ground level. He slowed down once he reached the bottom level, knowing that he was going to have to drive past the security booth.

He approached the booth and the guard hardly paid him any attention as he raised the security bar so that he could exit the garage. Once out onto the street, Jerry sped up heading for the freeway.

2

While Jerry was driving, he looked over at James again and seen that he looked as if he was ready to cry. Jerry knew that James had to be terrified by the fact that they were driving with an unconscious woman in the trunk.

They were on the freeway, when all of a sudden they heard a banging sound coming from the trunk.

"Shit! She must have awakened." Jerry said as he pulled over to the shoulder of the freeway. Jerry cut the car off, took the keys out of the ignition then exited the car. He headed back to the trunk and stuck the key into the lock.

He opened the trunk and was caught by surprise when Mary swung the same crowbar that he had attacked her with.

The crowbar hit him in his shoulder, which made a popping sound. A shocking pain went throughout his whole body.

Mary started to quickly scramble out of the trunk. Jerry took his right arm and grabbed his left shoulder, which had been knocked out of place. He winced in pain as he snapped it back into place.

Mary was out of the trunk and she went at him swinging the crowbar again. Jerry used his good arm and caught the crowbar in mid swing. He was trying to take the crowbar away from Mary as she fought him with her free hand as well as with her feet.

Jerry was forced to use his injured arm to try to restrain her. He grabbed her free arm, only to get bitten by her.

She clamped down on his finger and he yelled out in pain. Jerry was upset that James was sitting right there in the car and did not come to his aid. With both of his hands being full, he used his head to head bunt Mary. He banged his forehead against hers and she started falling to the ground.

She let go of the crowbar as she fell, leaving Jerry with total control of it. In a fit of rage he raised his arm and brought the crowbar down onto Mary's skull. He continued to strike Mary on her head with the crowbar until she was no longer moving.

She had been dead after the third blow, but he had continued to strike her, breaking her skull in many places.

When he got tired of beating her, he dragged her body down the embankment and into some bushes. Afterwards he went back to the trunk of the car.

When he had been acting as if he was rummaging through the trunk in the parking garage, he had noticed that James' medical bag was in there. He pulled the bag out and began going through it looking for a bandage and some adhesive tape.

While going through it he had come upon a bottle of chloroform. He knew that chloroform caused instant unconsciousness and wished that he had known that the drug was in the trunk before he encountered the woman.

He knew that he was not calling it a night until he found another patient. Figuring that the chloroform would prevent the same incident from happening again, he put the bottle into his jacket pocket.

He then pulled a bandage and a roll of adhesive tape from the bag. He bandaged his finger up, put the tape back into the bag then closed the trunk.

Jerry went and got into the car, then looked over at James, who was sitting in the passenger's seat breathing heavily.

The way James was looking let Jerry know that he had witnessed the whole thing. He thought to himself, "If I hadn't of taken the keys out of the car, the coward might have left me."

Jerry's face was in a mask of rage when he said to James, "That fucking bitch almost broke my shoulder! And she bit my damn finger! If you would have assisted me I wouldn't have had to go through all of that. Now I am forced to find another patient."

"I told you that I would not help you with the devilish things that you are doing." James replied.

"You are just a coward! You were a coward the day that I met you and you're still one now."

"What do you get out of hurting innocent women?" James asked him.

"They are weak and I get satisfaction from exposing their weakness."

"Just because they are women does not mean that they are weak."

With a sinister look on his face Jerry told James, "All women are weak. Think of your mother, she was weak and could not deal with the fact that your father left her. Her not being able to cope with him leaving is why she took her anger out on you. Think about your first foster mother. Do you actually think that she did not know what her husband was doing to you every time he entered your room? She heard your cries she just ignored them because she was too weak to do anything about it. And your wife James, she could not handle a little rough sex. She left you because she said you had perverted sexual ways that she could not deal with. Can't you see that women are weak and deserve to be punished?"

"You are not God and you have no right to determine who should and should not be punished."

"You're just a coward James a cold coward! The night is not over and I will find me another weakling."

James did not respond as Jerry put the key into the ignition and started the car. He sped off cussing under his breath, with all of his rage directed towards James, who sat staring straight ahead out the front window.

Jerry vented, "Your cowardly ways won't stop me from accomplishing my task." He drove for two miles then got off of the freeway.

He drove two blocks then pulled into a 24-hour Kroger's supermarket. The parking lot only had a few cars parked in it, being that it was after one in the morning.

Jerry spotted a Geo Prism that was parked by itself and decided to take a chance and park next to it. He cut the car off and took the keys out of the ignition.

He turned to James, "I'll be right back," he told him then got out of the car.

While walking towards the store Jerry looked back and saw James sitting up, stiff as a board. He smiled then turned around just as he reached the sliding doors.

He entered the store and walked the aisles looking for an easy victim. In the third aisle he spotted a young woman that was shopping by herself. Jerry stalked her as she went from aisle to aisle putting items into her shopping cart.

When the woman entered the aisle that held the spices, Jerry followed picking up a bottle of hot sauce. When the woman headed out of the aisle and over to the checkout line Jerry hung back. He pulled a handkerchief from his back pocket and took the chloroform out of his jacket pocket. He poured some of the chloroform inside of the handkerchief then he folded the handkerchief and put it back into his pocket. He put the chloroform back into his jacket then headed over to the checkout line.

He got in line behind the woman. The cashier was ringing up her items and he could tell from the amount of items that she had that it was going to take more than one bag for them.

He decided to strike up a conversation with her, "Looks like you are going to need some help with those bags." he said to her.

The woman turned around and looked at Jerry. She blushed when she seen a handsome man with steel blue eyes.

"I will be okay, it's not that much."

"I do not mind helping you. All I'm getting is this." he told her holding up the bottle of hot sauce.

"You came out this late at night for a bottle of hot sauce?"

"I'm just getting off of work and I have a plate of fried fish and rice at home waiting on me. I thought that I would grab me a bottle of Louisiana hot sauce on the way home to give it that Creole flavor. By the way my name is Jerry." The woman blushed again then said, "My name is Helen."

"Well Helen, my mother would be disappointed if she found out that I neglected being a gentleman, by offering you my help. Please allow me to assist you?"

The clerk had just finished filling up her second bag. Again, she blushed as she looked Jerry up and down. From his looks and the way that he was dressed she figured that he was not a psychotic or dangerous person.

She told him, "Thank you I appreciate it." She waited while the cashier rang him up and Jerry paid for his item.

Jerry put the bottle of hot sauce into his jacket pocket then picked up the heavier of the two bags.

Together they headed out of the store walking side by side. Once outside, Jerry asked her where she was parked.

"That's me over there." she said pointing to the Geo Prism. Jerry smiled inwardly, knowing that it was going to be easier than he thought.

He fell behind, letting her lead the way. While following her, he used his free hand to reach into his back pocket and pull out the handkerchief.

She walked up to the trunk of her car and inserted her key. She opened the trunk then sat her bag down into it. She then turned to Jerry, retrieved her other bag then again bent over to place the second bag into the trunk. While she was bent over, Jerry grabbed a hold of her upper body with his left arm. With the handkerchief in the palm of his right hand, he quickly put it over her nose and mouth. The woman never had a chance to react before she lost consciousness.

Jerry held her slumped body in his left arm as he used his right arm to close her trunk. He used both of his arms to drag her body to the back of James' car. He once again used his left arm to hold her, while using his right arm to open the trunk. When he got the trunk open he used both arms to put her into it. He closed the trunk then hurried back into the car.

When he got into the car, he looked over at James with an evil look on his face, "I told you they are weak. They are the easiest prey on this earth."

James did not even waste any words. He decided to remain quiet and not entice Jerry. Jerry started the car and pulled out of the parking lot humming a song to his self. He kept humming the song until he reached their home.

λ

Twenty minutes later Jerry pulled into the driveway of their home. He cut the car off and took the keys out of the ignition. He went to the back of the trunk, opened it and lifted the woman's body out. He shut the trunk and lifted the woman up into both of his arms. He started humming the same song again as he carried the woman up onto the porch. When he got to the door, he turned back to the car and seen that James was still sitting frozen in the front seat. He smiled at James, then unlocked the door and entered the house with the woman in his arms.

Once inside, he used his foot to kick the door shut then headed down to the basement where he had his private practice.

Once in the basement, he took his patient over to one of the triage rooms that he had sectioned off by plastic curtains. He placed her on the operating table and began removing her clothes.

The basement was a cross between a hospital's surgery room and a carpenter's workshop. Jerry had real operating tools as well as table saws, chain saws, routers and nail guns. He used both types of tools on his patients.

He could not wait for his new patient to wake up so that he could start operating. When he operated, he did not give his patients any numbing agents. He liked to see how much pain they could take before their bodies went into shock and shut down completely.

Jerry went into a small bathroom that was in the basement and changed into his doctor's attire. He put on some scrubs, some footies, a face mask and a pair of surgical gloves. After he finished he left out of the room smiling as he headed over to the operating table to begin to work on his patient.

3

The alarm clock brought Cody out of his sleep and out of a wonderful dream. He had been dreaming that he and Mary were making wild, passionate love. He was intending on making the dream become reality, when he rolled over reaching for Mary. His arm fell onto an empty space.

Cody sat up and said to his self, "Now where could she be?" He thought to himself, "Maybe she is in the shower." He looked down and seen that he had a full erection. He spoke to it, "Hold on buddy, we will find her. Let's see if the honeycomb hideout is in the shower." He got up out of the bed and headed out of the bedroom with his erection leading the way. He slowly walked to the bathroom, intending to surprise Mary.

He seen that the bathroom door was wide open as he approached it and he also noticed that he did not hear any running water or any other noise coming out of there. He went inside and stepped over to the toilet to relieve his self.

After emptying himself, he washed his hands then headed downstairs to continue his search for Mary.

"Mary, where are you?" he called out as he descended the stairs, but he got no answer in return. He got down the stairs and headed into the kitchen.

He found that it was empty. He walked back into the living room and stood dumbfounded, scratching his head. He was wondering where Mary could be. "Maybe it's a special occasion that I forgot about." he thought to himself.

Cody trotted back up the stairs and headed back into the bedroom. He entered the bedroom and grabbed his phone off of the nightstand. He looked to see if he had any missed calls and found that he had none. He also seen that the last time that Mary had called his phone had been at eight o'clock the night before, when she was on her break.

He dialed Mary's cell phone and after three rings it went to voicemail. He tried two more times and got her voicemail each time.

He wondered could she have gotten frozen at her job. Sometimes when the hospital was short on staff they would freeze an employee forcing them to work another shift.

He could not see that being done with Mary because she worked 12-hour shifts. To freeze her would mean that she would have to work a 24-hour shift.

Mary and her supervisor Lacey Williams were pretty close. Mary invited her over on many occasions, which allowed her and Cody to get to know each other pretty well. Cody decided to call up to Mary's job to see if she could tell him anything. He looked through his phone for the number to the hospital and when he found it he hit the call button.

When a receptionist came onto the line he gave her the extension to Mary's workstation. She put him on hold while connecting him to the receptionist that worked Mary's station.

When the receptionist came onto the line he asked to speak to Mary Weathers. She advised him that Mary was not in and was not do in for another half an hour. Cody asked to speak to the supervisor and was put on hold.

Minutes later Mary's supervisor, Lacey Williams came onto the line, "Hello?"

"Lacey this is Cody,"

"Hey Cody, how can I help you?"

"Mary did not come home from work last night and I was calling to see if maybe she was held over to work another shift."

"I'm sorry Cody, but Mary is not in. She is not due to come onto shift for another half hour. It's funny though, because I could of swore that I saw Mary's car parked in her parking spot down in the garage when I came on shift."

"What level of the parking garage?" he asked her.

"The third level, in the last row by the wall." she told him.

"Thanks," Cody told her, then hung up.

Cody knew that the only family Mary had in Cleveland was her sister Rachel. The rest of her family resided in Kentucky. He decided to call Rachel. He called her number, but got no answer. After trying the second time he decided to try Mary's best friend Bessy.

Bessy answered the phone sounding as if he had awakened her out of her sleep, "Hello?"

"Bessy this is Cody. I'm calling to see if you have heard anything from Mary. She did not come home last night and I'm worried."

"No Cody, I have not talked to Mary in a couple of days. Did you guys fall out or something?"

"No, it's nothing like that. For some reason she just did not come home last night and I have no idea as to where she can be."

"That's not like her Cody. Something has to be wrong."

"Yeah I know, I'm about to call the police."

"Have you talked to Rachel?"

"No, I called her number but got no answer."

"I can call up to her job. I think you should notify the police."

"I'm going to call them as soon as I hang up from you."

"Okay, you call them and I will call Rachel's job, then I will call you back."

"Okay," Cody responded, then hung up.

After Cody hung up from Bessy he called the police. He called to the Cleveland 2nd district police station and told the dispatcher that he wanted to report a person missing. The dispatcher put him on hold while connecting him to a detective. A detective came onto the line and Cody explained to him the situation. The detective told him that a person has to be missing for over 24-hours before a missing person's report could be filed. He informed Cody that if he did not hear from Mary by the next day that he could come down to the precinct to file a report.

Cody hung up the phone and started getting ready for work. After he was dressed, he called Bessy back to see if she had talked to Rachel and she told him that Rachel was in a meeting and that she left a message for her to call her back when she got a chance.

Cody told her that he had to go to work and that he would call her back when he got there. He looked at his watch and seen that if he did not hurry that he was going to be late for work. He grabbed his briefcase and quickly headed out of the house.

λ

James woke up at 10:30am and started getting ready for work. He went into the bathroom, where he brushed his teeth and took a shower. Afterwards he went back into his bedroom and started getting dressed. As he was getting dressed he started thinking about Jerry and the woman that he had carried into the basement the night before. He knew that she was probably no longer alive. None of them ever survived once Jerry had taken them into the basement and put them on his operating table.

He wondered where Jerry was and what he was up to as he headed out of his bedroom.

James went downstairs and into the kitchen. He went in there to make his morning cup of coffee. He filled the coffee pot with water put it on the stove then walked over to the cupboard to get a cup. While waiting on the water to heat up, he took in the fact that the house was eerily quiet. He had yet to see any sign of Jerry, so he went over to the door that led into the basement.

He opened the door and he was faced with complete darkness. He turned his head sideways and tried to listen for any type of noise indicating that Jerry was down there. He heard nothing but complete silence.

At the top of the steps there was a light switch and James hit it turning the lights on. He slowly descended the stairs holding on to the banister for support.

When he got to the bottom of the stairs he stood there for a minute just looking around. There was no sign of Jerry, but he noticed that one of the cubicles had the curtain pulled closed. Out of curiosity he walked over to the cubicle and pulled the curtain back and what he saw made his body go stiff.

James started to have a panic attack as he looked at the dismembered torso that was lying on the table. He could not believe that all was left from the woman that Jerry had brought home the night before was a completely dismembered torso. All of the limbs and the head had been removed from the torso.

James put both of his hands on top of his head and said, "Oh my God! What has he done? He is sick."

He wondered where Jerry was and what he had done with the rest of the body. He looked around the cubicle and notice that there was a garbage bag sitting on the floor at the back of the cubicle. The bag looked to be filled to capacity and was protruding oddly at different angles.

James walked over to the bag and seen that it was tied. He knew that it had to contain something that he did not want to see, but his curiosity would not allow him to leave the bag alone.

He reached down and untied the bag. He instantly became sick to his stomach when he came face to face with an eyeless, severed head.

Hollowed eye sockets stared out at James from inside of the bag and he got an overwhelming urge to vomit.

He let go of the bag and quickly covered his mouth. The bag started tipping over and he started backing up.

The bag fell over and the head rolled out of it. James knew that he was about to vomit, so he turned and started running for the stairs. He was trying to hold the feeling to vomit down until he reached the kitchen sink. He was three steps from the top when he found that he could no longer prolong the urge.

The bile rose up through his throat and forced its way out of his mouth. Vomit ran through his fingers as he headed over to the sink.

Once he got over to the sink, he removed his hand and bent over the sink. He continued to vomit, throwing up into the sink.

Once there was nothing left to come out of his stomach, he rinsed his mouth out and cleaned his hands. He was cleaning out the sink, when the urge to vomit hit him again, but he knew that there wasn't anything left to come out of him.

Feeling nauseated and dizzy, he decided that he needed to get out of the house. He heard the coffee pot whistling on the stove, and went over and turned the stove off.

He found that he no longer had a craving for coffee so he went and grabbed his briefcase, then headed for the door.

He jumped in his car heading to work. He was hoping that when he got in from work, that what he had saw in the basement would be gone. He knew that even if it was, what he had seen would never leave him. What he had seen would stay with him forever.

Cody got to his job forty-five minutes late. He knew that his supervisor would not complain. He worked as an insurance representative which allowed him to work a flexible schedule. He also knew that his supervisor Becky had a secret crush on him.

He was in his cubicle trying to look over some files, but he found that he could not concentrate, because he was worrying about Mary.

After an hour past he realized that he was not going to be able to get any work done until he figured out where Mary was.

He picked the phone up and called Bessy back and she answered the phone on the second ring, "Cody?"

"Yeah it's me, did you talk to Rachel?"

"Yes, I talked to her and she said that she hasn't talked to Rachel and does not have a clue as to where she could be. She sounded worried and said that she was going to call you."

Just when she told Cody that Rachel would be calling him, his cell phone began to vibrate on his hip. He pulled the phone from his hip and put it up to the opposite ear from the one that he held the business phone to. He took the call and found out that it was Rachel.

"Cody?"

"Yeah, hold on for a second," he told Rachel, then he spoke into the other phone, "Bessy, Rachel is on my cell phone right now. Let me talk to her and I will call you back."

"Alright," Bessy responded then hung up.

"Okay, I'm back Rachel."

"Bessy told me that Mary did not come home last night and that you have no idea as to where she could be."

"That's true, and I have called her cell phone several times and got no answer. Also Mary's supervisor told me that her car is still parked in the hospital's parking garage."

"You have to call the police Cody! Something has to be terribly wrong. There is no way that Mary would disappear without notifying one of us."

"I already called them, and they told me that I would have to wait 24 hours before I could file a report and they could start investigating."

"That is crazy! Their job is supposed to be to serve and protect, but they only become involved with a situation after something bad has already happened. I think me and you should go down there and raise some hell and maybe that will get them moving."

"We can do that! I can leave work right now."

"What station are you going to?"

"Second district,"

"Okay, I will meet you down there after I get out of my next meeting." They both hung up from each other then Cody grabbed his jacket off the back of his chair and headed out of his job.

4

Dr. James Mitchel was walking through the hallway of the Metropolitan hospital trying to calm his nerves.

Even though he had taken two valium pills earlier, he still felt like a nervous wreck. He was heading to his office to get two more pills out of the bottle that he had stolen from the pharmacy.

He held his head down as he quickly walked towards his office, because he was trying to avoid anyone that knew him for fear that they would try to stop and initiate a conversation with him.

He knew that he would not be able to hide his nervousness, because one of his patients had just inquired about why he seemed to be nervous. He had been trying to take the patient's temperature and the patient had noticed how badly his hand was shaking.

Dr. Mitchel had left the patient's room, deciding not to finish his rounds until he had gotten himself under control.

He was hurrying through the corridors, when he saw Dr. Rebecca Rogers standing by a receptionist workstation.

She had her back to him talking to a receptionist. Dr. Mitchel picked up his pace trying to make it past the station before she turned around and noticed him.

As if on cue and to his amazement as soon as he got to the workstation, Dr. Rogers turned around and said, "How are you doing James?"

James knew that he was busted, so he turned around with a fake smile on his face and replied, "I'm doing well, how are you Rebecca?"

"I'm doing well, I have just been wondering when is it that you are going to cash in on the rain check and allow me to take you out to dinner? The way you have been avoiding me, makes me think that you and your ex-wife have gotten back together."

"No we haven't gotten back together. I have just been tied up lately. I promise you that as soon as I have some free time that I am surely going to cash that check in."

Rebecca just stared at him for a few minutes. She took in how gorgeous he was and thought to herself he should have been a model instead of a doctor. She knew that most men models were gay and she wondered if it could be possible that Dr. Mitchel was gay.

Breaking out of her thoughts she said, "Okay," smiled at him then turned and started to walk away switching her hips.

As she walked, she looked back over her shoulder and said to him, "I'll be waiting." James watched her backside as she walked away and noticed that she had a nice enticing behind. He felt a stirring in his loins and when he looked down he saw that he was developing an erection. He used his clipboard to hide his erection as he quickly headed towards his office.

As, he was heading to his office, he found himself thinking about Dr. Rogers. He found her to be very sexy and wished that things could have been different. He thought to himself that under different circumstances it would have been him pursuing Dr. Rogers, instead of it being the other way around.

He knew that as long as Jerry was around that any female that he came in contact with would be in danger. He felt that he would not be able to live with himself, if his relationship with a woman brought harm her way.

James felt relieved when he reached his office. He stepped inside of it and was shocked when he saw Jerry sitting in his chair with his feet up on his desk. His nerves started to become more rattled and he quickly reopened the door.

He looked both ways, as if he was making sure the coast was clear. Satisfied that it was clear he shut the door back and locked it.

He turned back towards Jerry and seen that he had a sinister look on his face. James was outraged that Jerry was sitting in his office the day after he had kidnapped the woman from his job. He stormed over to his desk and yelled at Jerry, "What are you doing here in my office?"

"I came to check on you James."

"I don't need you checking up on me. You are the one that needs to be checked on. Matter of fact you need to be checked out by a psychiatrist."

"Why do you say that James?"

"I saw what you did to that poor woman."

"Ah, you visited my office and saw my exquisite work?"

"What I saw was the work of a demented per-son. How could you do that to that poor woman?"

"It was easy James I just took a power saw and began to dismember her. You should have been there to see the terror that was in her eyes when she realized what I was about to do with the saw. It wasn't until I had removed both of her arms and one of her legs, that the light in her eyes went dull."

"Stop it! Just stop it! I don't want to hear anymore. You are sick and I don't want anything to do with you and your demented ways. I want you out of my life!"

"Ah, come on now James. You can't mean that. You want to get rid of me after all I have done for you?"

"You have done nothing but make my life miserable. First you cost me my marriage, now you're trying to destroy me by getting me caught up in your wickedness. I feel like you are purposely trying to destroy me."

"How could you feel that way James? It was me who saved you from the life of torture that you were living in. It was me who dealt with them devils that were bullying you in high school. If it wasn't for me, you would probably be a fairy instead of a respected doctor."

"I never asked for your help!"

"You never turned it down either." Jerry told him.

"What can I do to get you out of my life?"

"There is nothing you can do. It's me and you forever."

"I can give you a way, by calling the cops."

"Go ahead and do it James. See what happens when they find out our little secret. Think things over carefully James, before you make a decision that could ultimately destroy your life."

"Get out!" James yelled at him.

Jerry removed his feet from the desk and stood up. James went over to the door and opened it. Jerry reached the door and stepped over the threshold. He turned back to James with his trademark sinister look on his face and said, "I have things to do anyway James. I must return home to remove my patient from the house piece by piece."

James slammed the door in Jerry's face then ran over to his desk. He felt as if he were having a panic attack, as he opened the desk drawer to retrieve the bottle of pills. When he grabbed hold of the bottle, a sharp pain went through his right hand. He held his hand up in front of his face and examined it. He noticed that his index finger was bruised. He tried to remember when he had hurt it, but his mind came up blank on how and when he had hurt it.

He took two more pills out of the bottle and took them without any water. He put the bottle back into the drawer then flopped down into his seat.

He put both of his hands up to his temples and started massaging them. He sat there trying to figure out how he could be done with Jerry for good. He wished that Jerry did not have the life destroying information to hold over his head. He also wished he could go back to the day he had accepted Jerry's offer.

The sedatives started to take effect and he laid his head back on the chair. His mind started drifting back to the beginning of his nightmare.

It started when the state found out that his mother was abusing him. They removed him and placed him in the care of some foster parents.

The events that appeared in his head happened over 23 years ago, but he could see them clearly in his mind. He was 12 years old living with a middle aged, childless, married couple. It wasn't long after he had arrived in the home that his foster father had started visiting his bed late at night.

His foster dad started to molest him on a regular basis. He always ignored James' cries as he forced himself on him. James would yell so loud that it had to be impossible for his foster mother not to hear what was going on.

James found himself trapped, with no family or friends to turn to. Jerry had befriended James and became the only true friend that he had. One day James confided in Jerry what his foster father was doing to him.

Jerry became enraged when he found out what the man was doing to his best friend and he came up with the plan to end all of the torture that James was going through.

One night Jerry switched places with James. He crawled into James bed and pretended to be him.

That night James' foster dad entered his room and climbed into his bed. He was surprised when instead of encountering the shy and timid boy he was met by a boy who had a crazed deranged look on his face. He also saw that the boy had a 10-inch butcher's knife in his hand. Before the man could climb back out of the bed, the boy began stabbing him.

The man screamed out in pain as he was viciously being stabbed. His screams had awakened his wife, who ran into the room to see what was going on with her husband. When she entered the room, Jerry jumped off the man and onto her. When Jerry was finished, both of James' foster parents were dead.

James had stood in shock watching what looked to be a scene out of a horror flick. After the couple was dead, Jerry used his electrical skills to set the house on fire. When the fire ignited, he and James quickly left the house.

James did not return to the scene until after the house had burned to the ground and the streets were flooded with fire trucks and police cars.

He approached the scene acting hysterical. He pretended as if he could not believe the scene that was before his eyes.

The police had questioned him about his relation to the couple that was found charred inside of the house. He told them that they were his foster parents. He expressed to them how good the couple was to him.

With tears running down his face, he told them how if he had not of went to the movies that he probably could have saved them.

The police explained to him how lucky he was to have been at the movies instead of in that house.

The fire marshal had eventually ruled the fire to be an accident. In his report he stated that the fire had been caused by faulty wiring inside of the fuse box.

James was placed with another foster family and him and Jerry had remained friends. They were the only two people that knew what had really happened to James' foster parents.

James second foster family had plenty of money and they took good care of him. They encouraged James to do well in school and to follow his dreams.

James decided that he wanted to be a doctor and they supported his decision. They paid James' tuitions through private schools, college and even through medical school. They even paid for his wedding when he and Melissa, who he met while in college, got married.

As thoughts went through his mind, he realized that it was because of Jerry that he was able to achieve his dream of being a doctor.

James felt grateful for what Jerry had done for him, but he just couldn't understand why Jerry wanted to destroy his dream that he had helped him achieve.

In his eyes it looked to him as if Jerry was trying to destroy him.

A vision of when things started going from good to bad between him and Jerry entered his mind. He and Jerry were still best friends and almost inseparable after Jerry killed his foster parents. James had found that he secretly had gotten a thrill out of watching Jerry kill his foster parents.

James knew that he did not have the guts to be a killer, but watching someone else kill a person excited him. He admired Jerry for being able to take another human life. After Jerry killed his foster parents, James had witnessed him use extreme violence on several occasions.

When James was in high school, he was being picked on by a group of boys that were seniors. Jerry found out what was being done to his friend and one night he asked James to take a walk with him. He did not tell James where they were going. They walked several blocks and when they got to a certain street Jerry pointed to a large tree and told James to duck behind it.

Once James was crouched behind the tree, Jerry crossed to the other side of the street. He hid behind a car as if he was waiting on someone to arrive. A few minutes later a teenage boy came walking down the street. Jerry peeked from behind the car and seen that it was the person that he was waiting for. It was one of the boys that were bullying James at school.

When the unsuspecting boy was walking past the car, Jerry jumped up and attacked him with a pocket knife. He stabbed the boy over 20 times. In the end the boy was lying on the ground bleeding profusely.

Before Jerry left, he pulled a note from his pocket and laid it on the boys bleeding chest. The note had read: "Take this as a warning your friends will be next."

After completing his task Jerry crossed the street, heading back to where he had left James. He got there and seen that James looked as if he was scared shitless. He told him, "Come on," and together they ran back to James' foster home.

None of the boys at school had ever bothered James again and Jerry had adopted the role of being James' protector.

For years they had remained close then James met Melissa. In his second year of college he met Melissa and fell head over heels for her. He started spending all of his time with her, which took time away from him and Jerry.

After falling for Melissa, James wanted to live a different life. Just like his foster parents, Melissa supported his dreams of being a doctor.

At the end of the fall quarter he proposed to Melissa and she accepted. They set a wedding date and when Jerry found out about it he became very upset. He felt that James was changing on him. One day he decided to voice his concern with James.

James heard him out, then explained to him that they would always be friends, but that he had a dream that he wanted to pursue. He told him that in order for him to make his dream come true, he was going to have to distance himself from Jerry and the things that he was doing.

To show good faith, he offered Jerry the role of being his best man in the wedding. Jerry turned his offer down and blamed Melissa for coming in between their friendship.

After James and Melissa were married, Jerry started to see less and less of James. He looked for ways to get Melissa out of James' life, so that he and James could be best friends again. He finally got his chance, when James confided in him about the problem that him and Melissa were having in their marriage.

Even though they hardly seen each other after James got married, Jerry was still the only true friend that James had.

So when Melissa told him that their sex life had become boring, James turned to Jerry for advice.

Jerry was more than happy to help James with his problems. He quickly gave James the answer, by advising him of the type of sex toys to buy and the type of things he needed to do during sex to bring their sex to life again.

James took his advice and at first things was going good. Every time he and Jerry met up, he would give him new things to try.

One night James went too far, when he strapped Melissa down on the bed. She was on her stomach and he rammed a 10-inch dildo inside of her rectum. Melissa had screamed out in pain, but James had ignored her pleas for him to stop, because he had mistakenly took them as screams of pleasure.

When he had finally let her up, she attacked him calling him an animal. She had to go to the hospital and get 13 stitches in her anus.

On the way home from the hospital, James had tried to console her, "Honey I'm sorry, I was just trying to spice up our sex life as you requested." Melissa was not having it she yelled at James, "What you have been doing for these past months has not been spicing up our sex life. The things that you have been doing are perverted and they only brought me pain instead of pleasure. You have become a sick pervert! You need to find you a whore to use your perversion on. I'm filing for a divorce."

λ

The next day when James arrived home from work, he found Melissa and all of her belongings gone. She filed for divorce and sued him for half of everything he owned. After the court granted her request James could no longer afford to pay the mortgage on the house along with the rest of the bills that was coming in. Jerry offered to move in and help him with the bills. James was leery about accepting his offer, because of his murderous ways. Jerry swore to James that he no longer had urges to do violent things to others.

James knew that he needed help with the bills so he took Jerry's word and allowed him to move in.

For the first six months Jerry seemed to be living a normal life to James. After the six month James started noticing that Jerry was displaying strange behavior. He would come home and find Jerry wearing one of his hospital coats along with wearing his stethoscope around his neck.

Sometimes when he came home, he would hear power tools being used in the basement. One day he decided to go down there to see what Jerry was up to. He found that Jerry had set it up to look like a doctor's office. He had created rooms that were sectioned off by curtains. He even had examination beds down there.

When James confronted him about it, he told him that he needed a place to work on his patients.

Little did James know Jerry was finding stray animals to take down into his so called doctor's office.

One day when James came in he heard power tools being used in the basement. He went down there to see what was going on. He pulled the curtain back on a cubicle, and seen that Jerry had cut off a cat's leg with a power saw. What really disturbed him was the fact that the cat was still alive and awake.

James had gotten the urge to vomit and fled back upstairs.

That was the first sign to him that Jerry had not changed. James knew that he should have separated himself from Jerry after witnessing that incident. He thought that whatever it was that Jerry was going through it would eventually go away.

He got the surprise of his life, when he entered the basement one day and found that Jerry had a human being strapped on his table. He had a completely naked woman strapped on the table. There was a huge amount of blood coming out of the hole where the woman's left breast use to be.

James saw tears running down the woman's cheeks, and he seen that the only reason she didn't scream was because Jerry had her mouth taped shut.

James had gone ballistic and he screamed at Jerry, "What the hell are you doing! I thought you said that you have changed?"

Jerry looked up with a sinister look on his face and replied, "I did change James. I'm now a doctor just like you and I'm operating on a patient."

"You're no doctor! You have no license to work on people."

"I'm just as much a doctor as you are and I do not need a license to perform on my patients."

"You're crazy! I want you out of my house now!"

"I'm not going anywhere James. Have you forgotten that I pay half of the bills? Have you forgotten what I did for you when we were kids? You wouldn't want me to expose our little secret now would you?"

After Jerry had threatened to expose their secret, James felt trapped and as time went on Jerry had used the same threat to get James to become more and more involved with his madness.

λ

Coming back to the present, James realized that if he did not find a way to break away from Jerry that his life would soon be destroyed. He looked at his watch, stood up and grabbed his clipboard. He left his office to finish making his rounds.

5

Cody had left work and was heading to the police station, when he decided to first stop by Metro hospital. He wanted to see if in fact Mary's car was parked inside of the hospital's garage.

When he got to the hospital he pulled up to the security booth that led into the garage. He paid the security guard the parking fee and the guard raised the guard bar allowing Cody to drive inside.

Cody drove up the circular ramp that led to each level and exited the ramp on the third level. He drove to the last row, where Mary's supervisor had told him she had seen Mary's car parked at. He was almost to the middle of the row when he spotted the car. There were cars parked on both sides of the car that looked like Mary's, so he pulled to a stop at the trunk of the black Taurus.

He exited his car and walked to the driver's side of the Taurus, where he leaned over and peered into it. He saw the exact same type of pine scented, tree shaped, air freshener that hung from Mary's car mirror. He took his hand, grabbed the door handle of the car, lifted it and found it to be locked.

He decided to go into the hospital and up to her workstation, to see if maybe Mary had shown up. He caught the elevator up to the sixth floor, got off and walked to her workstation. When he got there, the receptionist looked up, smiled then asked him, "How may I help you?"

"My fiancé Mary Weathers works here and I wanted to know if she has come on shift yet."

"Sorry, but Mary did not come in today."

"Could you call for Ms. Lacey Williams, her supervisor?"

"Sure, I can page her," the woman said to him then picked up the phone. She pressed a button that allowed her to send a page.

She paged Ms. Williams to come to station three on the sixth floor.

Cody stood at the station for about five minutes before a middle aged, slightly overweight woman appeared.

The woman approached Cody with a concerned look on her face.

"You had them page me Cody?" she asked him once she was standing in front of him.

"Yes I did, I still haven't heard from Mary and I just looked at that car parked in the garage and it does seem to be Mary's."

"I honestly do not know what to say Cody. I have not seen her and because she did not show up for work, we had to pull someone from another floor to cover for her. I asked other co-workers if they had seen her and they all said no."

"Something is not right, I'm about to meet her sister at the police station to file a report. I just wanted to stop by here on the way there, in hopes that she had shown up or called in."

"I wish that I could help you Cody, but Mary hasn't done any of those things."

"That's okay Lacey, thanks for your time anyway." Cody told the supervisor before turning to head back to the elevator.

Cody rode the elevator back down to the third level, got in his car and headed to the precinct.

When Cody got to the station he found that even with the stop he made at the hospital he still arrived at the precinct before Rachel.

He sat out in the waiting area for thirty minutes before a detective came out and escorted him to follow him. Cody followed the tall black man back to his cubicle.

Detective Mark Peterson was a forty-four year old homicide and missing person's detective. Peterson grew up in one of the roughest neighbor-hoods in Cleveland, Ohio and he had a no nonsense attitude when it came to his job.

When they got to his desk which was inside of a sectioned off cubicle, he told Cody to take a seat. Once he was seated, the detective introduced himself and asked Cody his name. Cody told him that his name was Cody Miller. After the introduction was made he asked Cody how he could help him.

Cody explained that his fiancé Mary Weathers had not come home from work the night before and how her car was still parked at her job.

The detective started asking him questions that made him feel offended. Detective Peterson asked him, "How is the relationship between you and Ms. Weathers?" Puzzled by the question Cody responded, "Our relationship is great!"

"Are the two of you in a committed relationship?"

"What type of question is that?" he asked the detective as he started to get upset.

"It's a good one, I'm trying to figure out if it could be possible that your girlfriend could be in the company of another man."

"Listen detective, yes we are in a committed relationship, we are engaged to be married."

"Tell me this, what do you suspect has happened to your girlfriend?"

"I don't know what to suspect, that is why I am sitting here with you. Isn't it your job to figure out what's going on?"

"Yes it is, but you have to give me a clue as to why you think your fiancé is missing, when the 24-hour waiting period for filing a missing persons report hasn't expired?"

"Fine, just listen to me for a second and you will understand my concern. My fiancé works at Metropolitan hospital. She works from twelve to twelve and got off work last night at midnight. She never made it home last night and this morning I called up to her job to see if maybe she had worked overtime. I was told by one of her supervisors that my fiancé was not at work, but that she noticed a car that looked like hers parked in the garage when she had come on shift that morning. I stopped by the hospital on the way here to see for myself if it was her car parked in that garage. I pulled to the spot that the supervisor had directed me to and found that it was indeed my fiancé's car parked there. The facts are she did not come home last night, her car is still parked at her job and no one has heard from her. I have tried her cell phone numerous times and haven't gotten an answer. I talked to her sister and closest friend and neither of them have heard from her. What else do I have to tell you to convince you that something is wrong?"

Peterson did not say anything, as he turned to his computer and pulled up the sheet used to file a missing persons report.

He was typing in Mary's information, when another detective led Rachel to his desk.

When they got to the detective's desk, Rachel saw Cody sitting there and asked him, "Have they told you anything yet?"

"No I'm filing a missing person's report right now." Peterson looked up at her and asked, "And who might you be?"

"I'm Mary's sister." The detective gestured for her to take a seat in the empty chair that sat next to the one that Cody was sitting in. She sat down and the detective began asking her questions, "What is your name?"

"Rachel Weathers?"

"Ms. Weathers, when was the last time that you saw or talked to your sister?"

"The last time that I talked to her was on Tuesday."

"When she talked to you did she give you any indication that she was planning to take a trip somewhere?"

"No she did not, the only place that we have family is in Kentucky and I called my parents to see if they had heard anything from her. They told me that they have not heard from her and they too are worried about her whereabouts."

The detective finished filling out the report and took down both Cody's and Rachel's information. He stood up then told them that as soon as he found something out that he would notify them.

He escorted them out of his cubicle and they headed for the exit. They were almost to there, when the detective called out to Rachel, "Ms. Weathers!" both Cody and Rachel stopped and turned around and Rachel responded, "Yes detective?"

"I would like to ask you one more question." Cody and Rachel both started walking back in the detective's direction when he called out. "I just need to talk to Ms.

Weathers, which made it clear to Cody that he did not want him there while he talked to Rachel.

When Rachel got back to the detective he asked her, "Do you know if maybe Mr. Miller and your sister have been having any problems in their relationship lately?" Rachel raised her eyebrows contemplating the meaning of his question then she told the detective, "Cody worships the ground that Mary walks on."

"Okay, I have no further questions." Rachel left back out of his cubicle and headed out of the station. Cody was standing right outside of the entrance when she stepped outside. They both started walking down the stairs and as they walked Cody asked her, "What was that all about?"

"He asked me about you."

"What could he possibly want to know about me?"

"He asked me were you and Mary having any problems in your relationship."

"What I ought to go back in there and clobber that guy."

"You would only be getting yourself into trouble Cody. He is just doing his job."

"I understand that but trying to make me into a suspect in her disappearance is not doing his job. He needs to get off of his lazy tail and get out there and find out what is going on."

They reached the sidewalk and Rachel turned to him and told him, "Well I'm heading home. I have to call my parents to give them an update. Call me if you hear anything else."

"I will," Cody responded as they took off walking in different directions. Cody got into his car and headed back to work.

6

Detective Peterson was sitting at his desk looking over the missing person's report for Mary Weathers, when his partner entered the cubicle. His Partner Detective Anita Perkins sat down at her desk, which faced his then asked, "What's that you're looking at?"

"Some guy just came in here and filed a missing person's report about his girlfriend. Detective Perkins antennas instantly went up. She had been working in the missing person's and homicide division for over seven years. In her experiences, most times when a boyfriend or spouse reported their significant other missing, they were usually the ones that caused them to be missing.

To her in actuality the person that filed the report was the only one that really knew the whereabouts of the so called missing person.

λ

Detective Anita Perkins was a 37-year old white female. She was divorced and had a 4-year old daughter. Detective Perkins had very deep issues originating from her past, that made her leery of all men.

When she was a child she watched in horror as her father, in an alcohol induced rage, viciously stab her mother to death. Perkins was only 5-years old at the time, but she knew that what her father was doing to her mother was hurting her. She had cried and begged her father to stop hurting her mother, but he ignored her cries and pleas as he continued to stab her mother to death. After he killed her mother, he walked past Perkins and out of the house in his drunken stupor.

Her father was eventually caught and pled guilty to aggravated murder. Little Anita had nightmares for many years and had to go to counseling.

Counseling had helped her and she had come out feeling better. She excelled in school and made the decision that she wanted to be a policeman.

After her mother's death she was placed in her grandmother's care. Her grandmother was proud of the way that Anita had gained strength and pulled herself together.

After finishing high school, she got accepted into the police academy. She was in the police academy and enrolled in college at the same time. While she was in the academy, she met Roger Perkins. She and Roger fell head over heels for each other and the day that they both graduated from the academy, they were married.

Three months into their marriage, Anita found out that she was pregnant. They were both happy about the pregnancy and when Anita reached her six month of her pregnancy she was transferred to a desk job.

Two months before their baby was born Roger got fired from his job, for not following safety procedures while chasing a suspect. He had been chasing a person suspected of robbing a bank.

Roger opened fire on the suspect as he fled down a busy street, and one of his bullets hit a 9-year old girl. The little girl died on the spot and after an internal affairs investigation, Roger found himself without a job.

After losing his job, Roger fell into a state of deep depression. Even the birth of their 7-pound, 4-ounce weighing baby girl could not bring him out of his depression.

Anita tried her best to cheer him up, but nothing worked. She found herself working an 8-hour shift, then having to go home and play maid. She would have to cook for Roger and tend to their daughter.

Roger started to become more and more de-pendent on Anita, and she found herself playing mother to both their daughter and Roger.

She thought that at least they could save money on hiring a baby sitter, by Roger watching their daughter while she was at work.

As time went on, Roger started to have violent out-bursts. He would vent his anger over losing his job by cursing no one in particular.

Anita found herself starting to get tired of Roger loathing in self-pity. She felt that he needed to get himself together and go find a job.

Things hit the fan, when she entered the house to the sounds of her daughter crying one night. She stepped through the door and seen Roger in a drunken state. He was sitting in a recliner chair, with his chin on his chest.

She looked at him with disgust as she quickly walked past him heading upstairs. When she got to the top of the stairs, her daughter's cries became louder. She hurried over to her daughter's crib and picked her up. Anita instantly knew what the problem was. Her daughter was soaking wet, and Anita could tell by the amount of wetness in the diaper that her daughter had wet herself several times.

She put her daughter to her shoulder and patted her back. She told her, "Shush, mommy got you," as she headed out of the room. She went to the bathroom where she wet a washcloth and grabbed a dry towel.

She went back into the bedroom and placed the towel on the bed. She then placed her daughter on the towel and commenced to changing her diaper. After she changed her daughter's diaper and she was no longer crying, she placed her back in her crib then went downstairs to deal with Roger.

She got downstairs and went over to Roger. She looked down at him and seen that he had saliva drooling from the corner of his mouth. She yelled his name out, "Roger! Roger!" but he did not move. She took her right foot and kicked his leg, "Roger get up!" Startled, Roger jumped out of his chair saying, "What's going on?"

"Why are you down here in a drunken stupor while our daughter is up there crying her eyes out, because she is soaking wet?"

"I did not hear her crying."

"How could you when you're down here drowning in your misery."

"Now wait a minute, don't you come in here sassing me. I'm the man of this house."

"Really! Do you really consider yourself a man? You don't work, you don't take care of this family. How do you consider yourself a man?"

"This is how," he told her before he hit her knocking her to the floor. He tried to advance on Anita and she scooted back on her behind, while using one of her hands to go for her revolver. When she got her gun out of its holster, she pointed it at Roger and he stopped in his tracks. Anita stood up then told him, "If you put your hands on me again, I will kill you!"

Roger sobered up real quick and tried to talk to Anita, "I'm sorry baby, and I did not mean to hit you. I just been under a lot of stress lately." Anita was not trying to hear nothing that he had to say. She had promised herself at a young age that she refused to go through what her mother had gone through.

She told him, "Get your shit and get out!" When Roger seen that she wasn't going to budge, he grabbed his car keys and left the house.

Two days later, Anita filed for a divorce. Be-tween what happened to her mother and herself, Anita grew a dislike for men. It took her over a year to warm up to her partner. She eventually learned that even though her partner was a homicide detective he really did not like violence. She had also learned that he was a devout Christian, and was married with three children.

She found that she had no choice but to learn to trust him. He was her partner and the one that was going to have to have her back out in the field. They had been partners since the first day she became a homicide detective. After three years of being partners she considered him as being more than her partner. She considered Peterson to be her friend as well.

λ

Peterson stood up and asked her, "You ready?"

"Where are we headed?" she asked.

"Up to Metro hospital, the boyfriend says her car is parked there." he told her as he headed for the door. Walking by his side she asked him, "How does he know that?"

"He said that he called her job and one of the supervisors told him that she seen her car in her parking space, when she had came to work."

"He real concerned huh?"

"He seems clean cut. The missing girl's sister showed up while he was filing the report. I pulled her to the side when they were leaving and asked her a few questions about him. She claims that he worships the ground that her sister walks on. She also said they were a happy couple."

"Wasn't Scott Peterson and his wife supposed to be a happy couple?"

"You have a point there Perkins." he told her as they climbed into their unmarked car and headed for Metropolitan hospital.

7

Dr. Mitchel got off work at 4:00pm. He exited the hospital through a door that led to the parking garage. Walking towards his car, he could see that there was someone sitting in the front passenger's seat of his car.

He knew that it could not be anyone but Jerry. His shoulders dropped and a gloomy expression formed his face. He dreaded having to deal with Jerry, because he knew that they would end up arguing.

He got to the car and went to unlock the door. He found that it was already unlocked and he climbed in. He looked over at Jerry, who was sitting there with a devilish grin on his face. James could not stand it when he had that look on his face, because it meant that he was up to something.

He said to Jerry, "I thought you were going home to clean up your mess?"

"I took care of everything James. My office has been cleaned spotless and is ready for the arrival of my next patient."

"Jerry, you are sick! You need to get yourself some help. When will you realize that you are not a doctor?"

"You may not see me as a doctor, but I am a highly trained surgeon."

"You and your madness are going to destroy me."

"James you have to relax. Have I gotten you in trouble thus far? Why are you starting to lose faith in me?"

"Because the way you think, and the things that you are doing are that of a sick and demented individual."

"You worry too much James. I have been taking care of you for years and now you are starting to lose faith in me."

"You damn right I'm starting to lose faith in you! You put me under the gun yesterday, kidnapping a woman from my job. What was that all about?"

"It was about you James. You have been changing and you have started to act as if you're better than me. I need you to realize that we are still a team, we are still one and the same."

"We could never be one and the same. You are a murderer and I'm a man that tries to save lives."

"At one time you did not have a problem with me being a murderer. You even said it yourself, that you got a thrill out of watching me kill people."

"Well things have changed and I'm living a different life now."

"There is no difference James. In your line of work and my line of work our actions decides who lives and who dies."

"I give up, I do not want to talk to you anymore. Nothing that I say gets through to you." For the remainder of the ride home neither of them said a word to each other.

λ

While James was driving his mind started to drift. He went back to the first time that he had helped Jerry with a kill.

James was in his freshman year of high school, when Jerry told him that he wanted to kill a prostitute. He told James that he needed him to lure a prostitute into an alley so that he could kill her. James had asked him why he needed him to lure her. He wanted to know why Jerry could not do it himself. Jerry told him, "I need you to do it because you look innocent. There is no way that I can get a whore to walk down a dark alley with me. All you have to do is proposition her and get her into the alley and I will take care of the rest."

James reluctantly agreed to assist him pulling off an act of pure violence.

When the night to carry the murder out came, James found himself to be both excited and scared. He was experiencing mixed emotions. He had witnessed Jerry killing his foster parents, but to watch Jerry kill an innocent unsuspecting person scared him.

Jerry tried to calm him down by telling him that everything was going to be okay. Before they headed up to the strip where the prostitutes solicited money for sex, Jerry instructed him on how to approach a hooker. He also told him what alley to lure the hooker to.

Together they walked up to the strip and when they got there, they stood on the opposite side of the street from where the hookers solicited their customers. Jerry picked out one then told James that he would meet him in the alley. They went their separate ways, with James crossing over to where the hookers were.

James approached the hooker that Jerry had pointed out. She was a tall blond with huge breasts. She had her back to him talking to a short brunette hooker. The brunette saw him approaching and told the other hooker, "We got a green one coming." The blond prostitute turned around and seen James approaching. Her eyes lit up, because she seen James as being a lick.

When prostitutes would come across square men, they saw them as easy prey. The hooker knew that if he picked her, that she would not have a problem rolling his pockets.

Both of them smiled when James reached them and the one that Jerry had pointed out spoke, "How are you doing honey?" James tried to speak but his words got caught in his throat. The hookers could tell that he was nervous. She told him, "Time is money sugar, what are you trying to do?"

James pulled a knot of money out of his pocket and the blond hooker's eyes lit up again. She said, "Now that's what I'm talking about, which one of us do you want. With all that money you can afford both of us." James pointed to the hooker that Jerry wanted. "I see you're smart, you picked nothing but the best. Where do you want to do this honey?" The blond asked him.

James pointed across the street to the alley. The hooker looked in the direction that he was pointing to. In her mind she thought that it was going to be easy. She thought if she sexed him in the alley, there wouldn't be any witnesses when she robbed him. "Suit yourself sugar," she told him, then grabbed his hand leading him across the street to the alley.

They walked side by side holding hands as if they were a couple. They entered the alley and the hooker seen that it was a big green dumpster in it. She led James behind it, so that they would not be seen by people walking by.

Once they were behind the dumpster, the hooker asked James, "You want it from the back?" James shook his head indicating that he did. The hooker turned towards the wall, and lifted her skirt up, which revealed that she did not have any underwear on.

She spread her legs, bent over slightly and placed both of her hands on the wall for support. She turned her head back, looked over her shoulder and seen James just standing there.

She told him, "Hurry up lover boy, I don't have all night." She turned back around and put an arch in her back, waiting for James to penetrate her. The next thing the hooker knew, she felt a sharp pain in her back. She tried to scream but no words came out.

The first strike severed her spinal cord and she crumbled to the ground. Jerry stabbed her 23 times before he stopped. He knelt down and put his hand over her nose and mouth to see if she was still breathing. When he was satisfied that she no longer had any life in her, he turned to James and said, "Well done," Together they quickly fled the scene.

James started coming out of his fog as he turned onto their street. Turning into their driveway, he thought about how since that first time, he had been involved in five other murders with Jerry. He figured that something dreadful must have happened between Jerry and a woman. He concluded that if he could find out why Jerry hated women so much that he could stop his madness. He shut the car off and he and Jerry walked silently up to the house.

8

Detectives Peterson and Perkins went up to Metro hospital and questioned Mary's supervisor and co-workers.

They all told them that Mary seemed fine and that she had punched out on time.

Peterson told the supervisor that Mary's boy-friend had told him that Mary's car was sitting in the parking garage, and then explained to him that when she came on shift she seen a car that looked like Mary's parked on the third level of the garage. She offered to show them where the car was and they accepted her offer.

They followed her to the elevator and rode it down to the third level. They exited the elevator and she led them to the car. She asked them if they needed anything else and they said no. They thanked her for her assistance and she headed back to the elevators.

Detective Perkins pulled out a pad and pen and wrote down the plate number on the car. She pulled out her phone and called the plate number in, while Detective Peterson walked around the car looking for clues.

Peterson went to the driver's side of the car and peered into it. He seen the pine scented air freshener that the missing woman's boyfriend had told him about. He went inside of his jacket pocket, pulled out a pair of rubber gloves and put them on. He did that so when the car was printed, his prints wouldn't be on it.

He grabbed the door handle and tried to open the car door, but he found it to be locked. He decided to look under the car for some clues. He knelt down on the side of the car and looked underneath it. When he looked towards the back of the car, he saw what looked to be a bag lying on the ground under the trunk.

He stood up, walked to the back of the car, and then knelt back down. He reached his hand under the trunk and retrieved what looked to be a lady's purse. He opened the purse and looked through it. In one of the inside pockets was a wallet. He pulled the wallet open, went through it and pulled out a driver's license. There was a picture of a woman on it and the name below the picture read Mary Weathers.

Perkins closed her phone and walked over to Peterson. She saw that he held a purse in one hand and some type of identification in the other, "I guess you already know it's her car?" Perkins asked him.

"Yes I do,"

"Where did you find her purse?"

"On the ground under the trunk,"

"We definitely have a missing person on our hands huh?"

"Hopefully, she is only missing. It looks like she dropped her purse during a struggle and the perp must have been either nervous or in such a hurry that he did not notice."

"So where do we start looking?" Perkins asked.

Peterson looked up and started scanning the garage looking for cameras. He only spotted one that was placed over the elevator. "You would think they would have more than one camera in an outside parking garage." Peterson stated.

"Maybe they don't have too much to worry about crime because of the security guard they have posted on the first level." Perkins responded.

"Well the camera looks like it's pointed this way, so let's go and check the security booth.

Peterson and Perkins caught the elevator down to the ground floor and headed to the security booth. There was an overweight white man sitting in the booth that had six TV monitors in it. When they got to the booth, Peterson pulled out his wallet and flipped it open so that his badge could be seen by the guard. The guard looked at the badge then up at Peterson. Peterson introduced himself, "I'm detective Peterson and this is my partner Detective Perkins. We are investigating a missing person's report and we would like to view footage from the camera that is mounted on the third level."

The guard pointed to the monitor that was getting live feed from the third level. Peters peered at the monitor from outside of the booth, but he could not really get a good look. He asked the guard if he could step into the booth to get a better look. The guard slid the door open and Peterson tried to enter. He found that the guard was too big for both of them to fit in there.

He stepped back giving the guard room to step out, and then he stepped in. Once inside he bent over and looked closely at the screen that the guard had pointed out. On the screen, the row in which the girl's car was parked couldn't even be seen. Peterson noticed that you could see the next row over and he seen people walking down it.

Watching the live feed, he got an idea. He figured if he viewed the footage from the night before, that he could possibly see somebody following her out of the elevator. He stepped out of the booth and asked the guard, "Do the hospital record these video feeds?"

"Yes sir, but you will have to go to the main control room to view them."

"And what floor would that be on?"

"It's right on the first floor. Just go to the front desk and they will direct you."

"Okay, thanks for your time." Peterson told the guard. He turned to Perkins, handed her the car keys, then told her, "You might as well get the car and call for forensics and a tow truck. I'm going to check out that video feed from yesterday."

"Alright," Perkins responded then headed for the car. Peterson headed inside of the hospital and approached the receptionist desk. Once again he pulled his wallet out and flipped it open, showing his badge.

When he got to the desk, the receptionist looked up and seen his badge.

"What can I help you with?" she asked him.

"I need to visit your main control room to view some video feed from the camera on the third level of the parking garage. It may help us in our investigation of a missing person."

The receptionist told him to hold on while she picked up the phone and dialed a number. She spoke into the phone for a few seconds then hung up. She looked back up at Peterson and said, "Somebody will be with you in just a minute."

Peterson decided to take some weight off his feet, by putting his elbow on the desk and leaning on it. Three minutes later, a hospital security guard approached the desk and the receptionist pointed to Peterson. Peterson introduced himself to the guard and told him what he was trying to do. The guard told him, "You can follow me."

Peterson followed the guard down a hallway and when they got in the middle of it, the guard stopped and pulled a set of keys out. The security guard opened a door that led into a corridor and he and Peterson entered it. Peterson stood looking around while the guard secured the door back. While walking in what seemed to be a semicircle, he realized that they were in between the walls.

The guard stopped at another door and opened it. He stepped aside and indicated for Peterson to enter the room. Peterson entered a room that was dimly lit. He saw that there were TV monitors lining the walls and that there were three guards manning them.

He noticed that each of the screens flicked every minute showing different areas.

The security guard that escorted him to the control room asked him, "What are you looking for specifically?"

"I'm looking for video feed from the camera that is over the elevator on the third level of the parking garage. Specifically, I'm looking for feed that was taking last night between 11:30pm and 12:30am."

The guard called over to another guard named Ralph, who was manning the monitor that received video feed from the camera on the level of the parking garage. He told him the date and time that he wanted him to rewind the video feed back to.

The guard hit some buttons on the control panel and the video on the screen started to rewind. At the top of the screen the date was shown and at the bottom of the screen the time was being shown in real time, Ralph stopped the video at 11:30pm the night before. Peterson stepped as close as he could to the monitor then asked Ralph to forward the video in slow motion. Peterson wanted to see if he could spot anything that could give him any clues as to what had happened to the missing woman.

As the video slowly moved forward he saw nothing out of the ordinary. The time on the screen read 12:13am, when he watched Mary Weathers come out of the elevator alone. He watched as she walked until she reached the turn off point for the row that her car was parked in. Once she made the turn that led to the row her car was parked in, she was out of the view of the camera. Peterson asked Ralph, "Is there another camera on that level?" Ralph answered, "No."

λ

"Did you find what you were looking for?" asked the guard that brought him in.

"Not quite, but thanks for your time and help anyway." The guard led him back out of the control room and back out to the receptionist desk. Again, Peterson thanked the guard, and then headed towards the door.

He walked back around to the garage entrance and headed up the ramp. When he got to the third level, he saw that the missing woman's car was sitting on the flat bed of a tow truck.

Perkins was talking to a forensics technician, who had dusted the car for prints. Peterson approached them and Perkins asked him, "Did you see anything?"

"Nothing that would be of any help." he replied.

"Well, the car has been dusted for prints and he is ready to take it to the investigation lot. What is our next move?"

"I say we go to the home that her and her boy-friend share and see if he can provide us with something that will be helpful." Peterson replied. What Peterson chose to do, set well with Perkins. To her the spouse of a missing person was the first one that needed to be ruled out as a suspect.

They got into their car and followed the tow truck down the ramp. When they exited the garage, the tow truck turned right and they turned left. They were heading to the address that was listed on the missing person's driver's license.

9

When Cody arrived home from work, he was surprised to see that the house lights were on. His mood instantly changed, because he thought that Mary had finally come home. As he put his key in the lock, he didn't know if he should be happy that she was finally home or be mad at her for pulling a disappearing act.

He unlocked the door, stepped into the house, then yelled out, "Mary!" He heard a door upstairs open and close then he heard footsteps coming down the stairs.

He stood with his hands on his hips, with an upset look on his face. He was surprised to see that it was Rachel and not Mary that was coming down the stairs. Rachel came down the stairs with a towel wrapped around her head and wearing nothing but a t-shirt. The shirt stopped at the middle of her thighs.

She walked over to the couch, flopped down on it then asked Cody, "Have you heard anything?" Cody was still shocked at her presence and the way that she was dressed.

"Cody!" she called out to him, bringing him out of the shock.

"Huh! Uh no!" Cody replied as he walked over to a chair, flopped down in it then replied, "No, I haven't heard anything. What about you? Did you talk to your parents?"

"They haven't heard from her, and they are really worried. I told them that I would call them back once you came home."

"How did you get in?"

"I still have an extra key that Mary gave me before you guys got together. I decided to come over here to wait on you to get here, to see if you have found anything out. I hope you don't mind that I took a quick shower?"

Slightly stuttering Cody replied, "Uh ... I don't mind, has anyone called?"

"Not so far," Rachel replied.

"I talked to Bessy and she said that she still hasn't heard from her." Rachel started to get choked up, "Oh Cody, do you think something bad has happened to her?"

"Honestly, I don't know Rachel. This is not like Mary to just up and disappear."

"Maybe you should call the police back and see if they have found out anything."

Cody got up from the chair and pulled the card out that the detective had given him earlier. He headed over to the house phone and picked up the receiver.

He started dialing the number that was on the card, when he heard a knock on the door. He put the receiver back on the hook and headed over to answer the door. He opened the door and was surprised to find the detective that he was about to call standing at his door with a white lady in a suit by his side. Cody glanced at the lady, but he kept his attention focused on Peterson.

Soon as the door had opened, Perkins had looked past Cody and took in the fact that there was a half clothed girl with a towel wrapped around her head sitting on the couch. Cody knew that the detectives were not there to give him any good news because Mary wasn't with them. Cody spoke, "What a coincidence detective."

"You care to elaborate?" asked Peterson.

"I was just on the phone about to call you."

"Yeah that's a big coincidence." Perkins stated with a smirk on her face. Cody finally turned his attention to the lady. He could tell she had an attitude and he did not intend to deal with it. He turned his attention back to Peterson and asked him, "Have you guys found out anything?"

"May we come in?" Peterson asked him.

"Sure," Cody replied as he opened the door all the way to allow them to enter. When they stepped into the house, Peterson immediately took in the fact that the missing woman's sister was sitting half naked in the house with her fiancé.

Cody closed the door behind them and they all stood there for a minute. Peterson broke the silence by saying, "I did not know that her sister stayed here also?" Cody knew that the detective was reading into what he was seeing wrong and he quickly tried to clear it up.

"Uh, she doesn't stay here. She just decided to come over, hoping that we could find out what's going on at the same time. As I said I was just about to call you to see if you had found anything out."

"Well, we did find this," Peterson told him as he lifted the purse up so he could see it.

"That's her purse, where did you guys find it?" Cody asked.

"We found it underneath the bumper of her car."

"Oh my God! Something has happened to her!" Rachel screamed as she jumped up off of the couch. When Rachel jumped up the t-shirt went up and both Perkins and Peterson got a chance to see that she did not have any underwear on. They looked at each other then Perkins asked Cody, "Does she plan on staying the night over here?"

"What! Who are you lady?" Peterson tried to take hold of the situation before it got out of hand.

"Mr. Miller this is my partner Detective Perkins and we came here to see if you could provide us with any other information that could help us locate Ms. Weathers."

"We would also like to know why your missing fiancé's sister is sitting up in here half naked." Perkins jumped in saying. Rachel gave Perkins a mean stare then responded before Cody could, "If it will satisfy your sick thinking, I will tell you why. I came over here so that I could be kept inside of the loop on information regarding my sister."

"That doesn't explain why you are sitting up in here half naked?"

"For your information, when I got here Cody was not here and after a long day at work I felt dirty, so I took a shower. Does that answer your question?" Rachel asked.

"Did you forget to put your clothes back on after your shower?"

"I was getting dressed when I heard Cody calling out my sister's name. I stopped dressing and ran down the stairs thinking that my sister was home. Does that satisfy you?"

"No, but it will do for now." Perkins responded. She continued to stare a hole through Rachel as Peterson took back over.

"Mr. Miller can you think of anyone that would want to cause harm to Ms. Weathers?"

"No! Mary did not have any enemies. Everyone loved her." Peterson turned to Rachel, "What about you? Can you think of anyone that maybe had it out for your sister?"

"No detective, Mary is the sweetest person that any-one could meet. I can't think of a soul that would want to do harm to her."

"Well if the two of you can think of something that could help us, please call that number on the card I gave you." Peterson told them.

Cody escorted them to the door and opened it for them. Perkins gave him an evil look as she walked past him. The way she was looking at Cody angered him and he asked her, "What is your problem lady?"

"I don't have a problem, none at all." she said to him as she crossed the threshold. After closing the door, Cody turned to Rachel and asked her, "You do plan on leaving tonight, don't you?"

"I did have plans on staying until we got news of my sister's whereabouts."

"I don't think that would be a good idea Rachel."

"Cody, don't tell me your letting them detectives get under your skin. For God's sake you're my sister's fiancé. I have no interest in you."

"I know that, but the police don't see it that way."

"Fine, I will leave then, she told him, then jumped up and headed upstairs." After ten minutes, she came back downstairs fully dressed. Cody led her to the door, opened it then told her that he would call her as soon as he heard something.

10

Peterson and Perkins were heading back to the precinct and were both trapped in their own thoughts, Perkins looked over at Peterson and asked him, "You don't think it's strange that a missing girl's sister is sitting up half naked in her home with her boyfriend?"

"Yes, I find it somewhat strange, but it doesn't prove that they are involved in any foul play."

"I guess you are right, but only time will tell." she responded then fell silent for the rest of the ride to the station.

Peterson had intentions of getting back to the station, filling out his report, then heading home. He soon found that things weren't about to go according as planned. When he and Perkins entered the station, the desk sergeant called them over.

"Peterson, Perkins, we have someone here trying to file a missing person's report." The sergeant turned and called out to an older woman, "Ms. Morgan, you can go with these two. They are going to take your report.

Peterson and Perkins turned and seen an older woman with two kids, one flanking each side of her.

Peterson looked at his watch, and then frowned. He knew that he wasn't going to get off on time. There was no way he could get two reports done in forty five minutes.

Perkins picked up on his facial expression. She knew that he wanted to get home to his wife and she figured that she could take the report by herself.

"Go ahead and fill out the report on Weathers and I will handle this." she said to Peterson. Then she turned to the old woman and told her, "Follow me ma'am." Peterson led the way with Perkins behind him and the woman with the two kids pulling up the rear.

When they got to their desk, Peterson booted his computer up to work on his report on the Weathers case. Perkins sat at her desk and told the old woman to take a seat in the chair that was next to the desk.

Perkins started taking the woman's missing person's report. She pulled up the missing person's sheet on her computer then turned to the woman. "Okay ma'am, could you tell me who it is that is missing?"

"It is my daughter,"

"And what is your daughter's name?"

"Her name is Helen Morgan."

"When was the last time you seen your daughter?"

"Last night,"

"And why do you think she is missing?"

"Because she left out of the house last night to go do some shopping at the 24-hour Kroger's supermarket and she never returned."

"Do you and your daughter live in the same residence?"

"Yes,"

"Do you think it is possible that your daughter could be in the company of a boyfriend?"

"Helen doesn't have a boyfriend and she wouldn't go anywhere for too long without checking on her children."

Perkins looked at the two children that flanked both sides of their grandmother and she seen the sad looks on their face.

The old woman's story got Peterson's attention and he looked up from his computer and over at her and her grandchildren. He saw the sadness in the faces of both the old woman and her grandchildren.

One thing Peterson dreaded was seeing the pain and despair in a person's eyes, when a love one has become missing or found dead. Something about seeing the old woman and her two grandchildren with sad looks on their faces tugged at his heart. After seeing that, he knew he wasn't getting off on time that night. He decided to ask the woman a few questions himself.

"Excuse me ma'am, could you tell us what time was it that your daughter went shopping?"

"It was about one in the morning."

"Does your daughter usually do her shopping in the early morning hours?"

"Helen works in the day time, plus she doesn't like to shop at the times the stores will be crowded. She finds it more convenient to do her shopping at night."

"Could you tell us which Kroger's your daughter went to?"

"She always shops at the one on West 150th and Brook Park."

"What type of car does your daughter drive?"

"She drives a dark blue Geo Prism."

Peterson looked up to make sure that Perkins was taking everything down and found that she was.

"One last question Ms. Morgan, do you happen to have a picture of your daughter with you?"

"I think I have one of her with my grandchildren." she replied then opened her purse. She went inside of her purse, pulled out her wallet and removed a photo. She handed the photo to Peterson, who looked at it.

He saw a picture of a pretty blond woman sitting with the two children that were standing before him. He looked over to the missing woman's children again and noticed that the little girl, who was about eleven had tears forming at the corner of her eyes. She looked at Peterson and asked him, "Are you going to find my mommy?"

Even though he was not sure if he would indeed find her mother, he told her, "Yes, I am going to try my best to find her and bring her back to you." He then turned back to the grandmother and asked her, "Do you mind if I hold on to this photo? It could be real helpful in our investigation."

"God yes, if it will help you find my child you can have it." she said emotionally.

Perkins resumed talking to the grandmother. "Ms. Morgan we are going to investigate this to the fullest. If you think of any more information that may be helpful to us, please call the number on this card." Perkins handed the lady a card that had their number on it. The old woman got up and Peterson escorted them out.

When Peterson got back to his desk, Perkins said, "I know you want to get home. We can put this on the agenda for the first thing tomorrow."

"Tomorrow might be too late. If I had someone missing, I wouldn't want the search to be put off. We might as well go up to the Kroger's and see what we can find out." he told her as he lifted his jacket off the back of the chair and put it on. "Lead the way," Perkins replied then followed him out of the station.

They drove out to the Kroger's supermarket. When they got there, Peterson circled the parking lot looking for a dark blue Geo Prism. He went around the lot twice and did not see any car that matched the description of the car belonging to the missing woman. After he circled the lot a second time, he pulled to a stop in front of the store. He cut the car off and turned to Perkins, "We might as well check inside and see if someone that works here can tell us anything." They both got out of the car and headed into the store. While they were walking Peterson reached into his coat pocket and pulled out the picture that he had gotten from the missing woman's mother.

When they got inside the store they saw that it was almost empty. There was only one cashier on shift and Peterson and Perkins approached her. The cashier was busy reading a magazine when he approached her. She wasn't even aware of the two detectives standing at her counter. Peterson pulled out his wallet and flipped it open so that his badge was showing. He read the cashier's name off of her name tag, then spoke, "Excuse me Ms. Gibson." Startled, the clerk let the magazine slip from her hand. She bent down and picked it up. Then she stood up, and looked at Peterson's badge and asked, "Can I help you?"

"I'm detective Peterson and this is my partner detective Perkins." We are investigating a missing person's report. The missing person's mother says that her daughter was supposed to be here shopping the night she went missing. Could you look at this picture and tell us if you remember seeing her here last night."

"I can look at the picture, but I was off last night. You would have to see Gary, because he was on shift last night."

"Could you still take a look, because her mother said that she shops here often." Peterson told her as he held the picture out to her.

"Sure," the cashier replied then put her hand out to accept the picture. She looked at the picture and raised one of her eyebrows. Peterson could tell from her facial expression, that she recognized the woman.

"Yes, she does shop here frequently and it's mostly at night."

"And you say Gary was working last night?"

"Yes, it was Gary who worked last night."

"What is Gary's last name?"

"It's Chambers,"

"Do you have a number for Gary?"

"No I don't, you will either have to see the manager to get his information, or come back up here tomorrow night and see him personally."

"When does the manager come in?"

"At 7:00am,"

"Okay thank you for your help." Peterson told her.

"You're welcome; I hope that you find out what happened to her. She seemed like such a nice lady."

Peterson took in her last remark as him and Perkins turned and headed out of the store. They got into their car and headed back to the station. While driving, Peterson turned to Perkins and said, "It's been a long day. We might get about four hours sleep, before it will be time to punch back in."

"The way they work us the precinct should do like the firehouses and put beds in the station for us."

"Ha Ha! No thanks, I like being in the comfort of my own bed, with my lovely wife at my side." After hearing Peterson's comments Perkins fell silent. What he said about being with his wife had struck a nerve. It made her think about how lonely she had become since her divorce from Roger. She silently wished she could feel the comfort of having a man in her life. She knew that she would soon have to deal with her issues regarding men, or she would forever be lonely.

They got back to the station, clocked out and went their separate ways. Peterson was going home to his wife and Perkins was on her way home to spend another lonely night in bed.

11

Detective Perkins arrived at work the next day and was notified that the body of a dead woman had been found on the side of a freeway. The captain informed her that the case was being given to her and Peterson.

Peterson arrived at work fifteen minutes after Perkins. When he pulled into the station's lot, he already had the day's schedule in his head. His first plan of the day was to return to the Kroger's supermarket and talk to the manager. For the second time in two days, he found that things don't always go as planned.

When he arrived at his desk, Perkins still had her coat on and a steaming cup of coffee in her hand. He went to sit down and she said, "There's no sense in sitting down. The captain just told me that a body was found on the side of the 480 freeway. He wants us to get there pronto."

"I don't even get to have my morning cup of coffee?"

"I took care of it for you. It's just how you like it, straight black with two sugars," she told him as she handed him the cup of coffee.

"Thanks," he told her then accepted the coffee. He took a sip then perked up. He said to Perkins, "You should be working at Starbucks®."

"Very funny!" she replied as she led the way out of the station. They left the station heading to the crime scene. While Peterson was driving, Perkins was flipping through her notes. Peterson asked her, "Who found the body?"

"They said some community service roadside workers."

"We have two missing persons in one day, now a body has been found. What are the chances that the body could be one of the missing women?" Peterson asked Perkins.

"I say it's a high probability, there has been no other report of a female missing lately."

"Well for their family's sake let's hope it's not one of them." Peterson stated as he drove up the ramp leading to the 480 freeway. They were driving for no more than ten minutes when they saw a large gathering up ahead on the side of the freeway.

"Looks like every news station is out here." Perkins stated.

"Yes, it definitely seems that way." replied Peterson as he pulled over to the shoulder of the freeway. He dreaded getting out of the car, because he knew that they were going to be swarmed by the news media. They were going to want answers in a case, in which the facts weren't even in yet.

He turned to Perkins, "You can do the honors of being the PR rep today. I don't want nothing to do with them."

"Well thanks for offering to throw me under the bus." Perkins replied as she got out of the car.

The reporters had been out there over an hour, trying to find out what happened to the dead woman and who she was. The Cleveland police department had used sticks and yellow tape to keep the reporters out of the restricted area.

Soon as the reporters seen Perkins exit the car they swarmed her sticking their microphones in her face. They all started shooting questions her way at the same time.

Peterson got out of the car and walked around it to join her. He pushed through the crowd of reporters telling them, "We have just arrived on the scene. You guys know more than we do. Now please move out of our way, so that we can do our job."

He continued to push through them until he reached the yellow tape. He stepped aside and lifted the yellow tape so that Perkins could duck under it. He ducked under it himself and together they carefully walked down the embankment.

They got down the embankment and seen uniformed officers congregating. The body was further into the wooded area and they walked into it. When they entered the area, they noticed the unusual amount of flies that were swarming. They found out why when they got two feet inside of the wooded area. The woman's rapidly decomposing body was on the ground with a sheet covering her. The decomposition was attracting the flies. It was mid-July and the high temperatures had caused the woman's body to decompose at a faster rate than it usually would have.

Peterson and Perkins saw two CSI workers standing next to the body, talking to the coroner. They approached them and introduced themselves. After the introductions were made, Peterson set out to find out what the investigators had discovered so far. Peterson started asking questions, while Perkins took out a pen and pad to take notes. Peterson directed his question at the investigator, whose nametag read McIntosh.

"So McIntosh, what do we have here?"

"We have a dead female that looks to be any-where between the age of twenty-five to thirty. She looks to have been beaten repeatedly upon her head with an object that was heavy enough to crack her skull in multiple places."

"Did she have identification on her?"

"There was no ID found and because of the rapid deterioration, it may be hard to get a good identification."

"Can you give an approximate time of death?"

"Well, even with that rapid decomposition, I would say she was killed no more than two days ago."

"Is there anything else that you can give us?" Peterson asked him.

"Yes, she fought with her attacker. We found skin under her finger nails and inside of her mouth."

"So she scratched and bit the perp?"

"That's what it seems like."

"At least she was a fighter and left some clues. How long is it going to take you to analyze the DNA?"

"Give us two days and it should be done. We will also put it in our database to see if we come up with a match."

"That will be very helpful. Please call us if you find a match?"

"I sure will," the investigator told him. They shook hands then Peterson was ready to go see the body himself. Together he and Perkins walked over to the body. Perkins used her notepad to try and chase the flies away and Peterson knelt down and lifted the sheet from the dead woman's face.

"My God!" Peterson stated loudly when he observed how the whole right side of the woman's skull was caved in. He pulled the sheet away some more so that Perkins could get a look at the results of what had to be pure violence.

She told Peterson, "That looks like the work of someone who had a real vendetta against her."

"Either that or they got angry, when she decided to fight back."

"Whichever it may be, the perp has to be one sick individual. Do you think it could be one of the missing women?"

"It's hard to tell from looking at this side of her face." Peterson replied. He stood up, reached into his back pocket and pulled out a pair of latex gloves. After putting the gloves on he knelt back down and turned the woman's head from the right to the left side. He reached into his inside jacket pocket and pulled out the photos of the missing women. He looked at the first picture, then at the dead woman and found that there was no need to look at the other picture. He was saddened by the fact, that the body was indeed that of one of the missing women.

He looked up at Perkins with a gloomy look on his face. "Which one is it?" she asked him knowing from the look on his face, that it was one of them.

"I'm afraid it looks like Mary Weathers. But we need to wait on the DNA on the body or dental records to be sure."

"CSI said that she fought her assailant and left distinguishing marks on him. I don't remember seeing any marks on the boyfriend, do you?"

"No, I don't recall, but if the marks are on his chest area they wouldn't be visible anyway." Perkins stated.

"If it does turn out to be Mary Weathers, I say we ask her fiancé to take a DNA test." Peterson did not respond to her last comment. He knew that she still had unresolved issues with men. They both stood there and watched as EMT workers lifted the body, carried it up the embankment and loaded it into the coroner's van. The news crews were still there and wanted answers.

A reporter from channel eight news approached Peterson and Perkins and began asking them questions, "Detectives, do you have a positive identification on the woman that was found?"

"No, we have to wait on the DNA results or the dental records to find out who the victim is." Peterson told them. Channel five news jumped in with a question, "Could you tell us how the victim was killed?"

"That information cannot be released at this time."

"Do you think this is the work of a serial killer and this body may be the first of many you will find?"

"There is no evidence that this is the work of a serial killer, listen this investigation is still in the beginning stages, when more facts are found out the media will be notified. Now if you will excuse us we have work to do."

Peterson parted the reporters and he and Perkins got back into their car. Peterson told Perkins, "Since we are already on the freeway, we might as well head back over to Kroger's."

"You're doing the driving." Perkins responded.

Peterson drove to West 150th, to revisit the Kroger's supermarket. When they got there they went inside in search of the manager. They went to the first checkout counter, where Peterson did as usual, flipping his wallet open and showing his badge.

He told the cashier that he wanted to see the manager. The cashier paged the manager and he arrived in less than two minutes. Peterson introduced himself and Perkins to the manager and then he told him that he needed some information on one of his employees. The manager told him and Perkins to follow him and he led them to his office. When they got inside, he sat behind his desk and told them to have a seat in the two chairs that were in front of his desk.

Once they were seated, he asked them, "So what is this all about?"

"We are investigating the whereabouts of a missing woman. Her family believes that this store was her destination, when she disappeared."

"When was it that it took place?"

"It was the night before last, at about one in the morning."

"Okay, so what do you need?"

"Well, we visited here last night and talked to one of your cashiers. I think her name was, uh." Peterson got stuck trying to remember the cashier's name and Perkins jumped in saying, "I got it," she flipped open her notebook and turned to the page that had Mary Weathers' name at the top. "Her name is Tasha Gibson."

"Thank you," Peterson said to her then turned his attention back to the manager. "Ms. Gibson said that she was not on shift the night before last. She advised us that we would have to talk to a Gary Chambers. We wanted to know if you have a number or an address on him so that we may get in touch with him."

"We keep a file with all of our employee's numbers and addresses on it. Hold on for a second, I will get it for you." The manager went over to a file cabinet, opened one of the drawers and went to the section that listed the last names that began with the letter C. When he found Gary Chambers' file, he pulled it out and said, "Here it goes right here." He went back over to his desk, sat down and flipped the file open. He said to Perkins, "I see you are always prepared. Do you care to write this information down?"

"Sure, go ahead and read it off." she replied. The manager read off Gary's number and address. After they got the information, the manager was escorting them out of his office, when he remembered something. He stopped and turned around, causing Peterson and Perkins to stop in their tracks.

"Detectives you say this woman came up missing the night before last?" Peterson and Perkins stopped in their tracks and Peterson said, "Yea, the night before last. Why do you ask?"

"Well we had to call a tow truck yesterday to come remove a car that was parked in a handicap spot, with no sticker on it. We did numerous pages asking for whoever owned the car to move it and no one responded to the pages and no one ever laid claim once the car was towed."

"What type of car was it?" Peterson asked him.

"I know that it was a dark color and the name of it was G ... O something."

"You mean Geo Prism?" Perkins asked him.

"Yes, that's the name I was looking for." the manager said getting hype. It made him feel good to be of some help to law enforcement. Peterson and Perkins looked at each other then Peterson asked the man do you know what lot the car was taken to?"

"I believe it was taken to the lot downtown across from the football stadium. That is the lot where most cars that get towed from here go."

"Thank you for your time. You have been a big help to us." The manager beamed with pride as he shook both of the detective's hands. Peterson and Perkins left the supermarket heading to the tow lot.

12

James was sitting in the hospital's break room, nursing a cup of coffee. He was staring at the television that was mounted on the wall. The television was showing the twelve o'clock news and even though it looked as if he was watching the television, his mind was really somewhere else.

He sat there thinking about how much his life had been turned upside down. He did not know if he should place all of the blame on Jerry or accept some of the responsibility himself. He knew that he was not totally innocent in all of the events that had taken place in his life. He tried to rationalize as to why he allowed himself to be involved in the madness that Jerry had been doing since they were kids. He needed a way to justify his actions, so he started thinking about the things that Jerry kept trying to get him to believe.

Jerry told him that all women were weak and deserved to be punished. He told James that his mother had been weak and as James sat there reflecting on the past he could see Jerry's point. His mother beat him repeatedly for no reason at all. James sat there thinking about how a mother is supposed to give her child her unconditional love, but his mother only gave him slaps to the face.

Next, Jerry had told him that his foster mother was weak and as James looked back he could definitely see that she was. In his mind he knew that she had to know what her husband was doing to him. He figured that either she did not care what her husband was doing to him or she was too scared to do something about it.

Last thoughts of his ex-wife, came into his mind. James thought about how he had only tried to grant her wish. He reflected on how it was her that brought it to him that she wanted to spice up there sex life. In his head he concluded, that she was indeed weak for not being able to handle a little rough sex.

As he sat there and continued to reflect, he tried to come to terms with all that had happened in his life. He needed to know if what he went through, justified what he had let himself become involved in with Jerry.

Before he could decide, words from the TV anchor on the television caught his attention. James tuned in to what the anchorman was saying, "After the break, I will bring you news of a woman that was found dead this morning on the side of the 480 freeway." After the anchorman's synopsis the television went to a commercial.

James body started to tremble as he realized that it was probably, the woman who Jerry had killed. He became anxious, as he waited for the commercials to end. He desperately wanted to find out what they knew about the woman's death.

To James it seemed as if the commercials would never end. He found himself becoming nervous and he started perspiring profusely. He noticed that his hands were shaking and he decided to put them both onto his coffee cup. He did that in order to prevent the other doctors and nurses that were in the break room from noticing how bad they were shaking.

The news finally came back on, and James sat upright, giving the television his full attention. The anchorman started giving his report, "Now for our top story. Earlier this morning a woman's body was found, in a wooded area near the 480 freeway. Our correspondent, Terry

Edwards is live at the scene," The screen split in two, allowing the viewers to see both the anchorman and the correspondent that was live on the scene. Viewers could see that there were a lot of reporters at the scene and behind them the viewers could see that there was yellow tape being used to rope off the area.

When the television started showing the scene, James' hands started shaking so bad that over half of his coffee spilled over the rim of the cup. He nervously looked around the room making sure that there wasn't anyone watching him. When he was sure that there wasn't he turned his attention back to the television.

The anchorman started to inquire about the woman from the correspondent, "Terry are you there?"

"Yes, I'm here Rick."

"Terry, could you tell us about the gruesome find at the scene behind you?"

"Well Rick, the body of a dead female was found about seven thirty this morning."

"Could you tell us who found the body?"

"Yes, some community service workers that were cleaning the sides of the freeway found the woman. Her body was found in a wooded area down this embankment located right behind me." The camera briefly left the reporter and showed the embankment, leading into the wooded area.

When the camera went back to the reporter, the anchorman resumed his questions. "Terry have authorities positively identified the body yet?"

"No, not as of now, there was no identification found on the body. A source within the police department informed us that because, of the scorching hot summer weather the body has started to rapidly decompose. He says that it is going to take DNA testing to positively identify the body."

"Terry, I know that the body has already been removed from the scene, but do we have video footage, of the body being removed?"

"Yes Rick, video feed was sent to the station earlier."

"Hold on Rick, I just got word that the footage is ready to be shown." The image of the correspondent left the screen and was replaced by a video clip of the body being carried to the coroner's van. After the body was shown getting loaded into the van, the video feed of the correspondent came back onto the screen. The anchorman directed more questions to him, "Terry did authorities give any indication as to how the woman was killed?"

"No they didn't Rick. They say the investigation is still in the beginning stages and that as they gather more facts, they will provide us with more information. As of now, law enforcement wants anybody who may have information regarding this murder to contact Crime Stoppers at (216)555- 7875."

"Okay, thank you Terry." The picture of the reporter left the screen and the full picture of the anchorman was being shown again. The anchorman then spoke to the viewers, "As more facts come in, we will continue to give updates. Now let's go to Ron Hightower for traffic."

When the news clip about the woman ended, James jumped up and headed to his office. He decided that he was going to call it a day. When he got to his office, he called another doctor and asked him to cover for him. The doctor agreed to cover for him for the rest of the day and James got all of his things together. He left work, heading home to confront Jerry.

Peterson and Perkins arrived at impound lot #3. They went to the office and asked to speak to the person that was in charge. They found that the old man with the oil stained overalls on standing before them was the person in charge. Peterson showed the man his badge then asked him what his name was. The man told him to call him Mike.

Peterson addressed him by that name, "Mike, I'm detective Peterson and this is my partner detective Perkins. We are investigating the disappearance of a woman. We believe that her vehicle was impounded to this lot yesterday."

"What type of car is it?" asked Mike.

"It is a dark blue Geo Prism and it was towed from the 24-hour Kroger's up on Brook Park Road."

"I remember that car, I think it's parked in row six, let me check." Mike started flipping through a rolodex that was used to keep records of the cars that were impounded to the lot. After a few seconds he said, "Just as I thought, hold on a second." He took what looked to be a two way radio off of his hip and spoke into it, "Charlie come to the office."

A few minutes later a man that was black as the midnight sky and looked as dirty as a junk yard dog appeared at the office door. Mike told him, "Take these here detectives to that car that came in yesterday. The blue Geo Prism, that's sitting over in row six."

"I got them," he replied, then turned to the detectives and said, "You guys can follow me."

Perkins cringed at the site of his mouth. Charlie was missing at least four upper and bottom front teeth. They followed Charlie through the impound that looked more like a junkyard. The lot was covered with loose gravel and dirt and every time a gust of wind would blow the dust flew up in the air. The dust effected Peterson's allergies. He could not control his sneezing and coughing. He pulled a handkerchief from his back pocket and put it over his nose and mouth.

When they got to the sixth row they turned down it and found that the Geo Prism was the third car on the left.

Perkins pulled out her pad and pen and immediately took down the plate number. Peterson removed the handkerchief from his nose and mouth so that he could put on another pair of latex gloves. He walked around the car checking to see if any of the doors were unlocked. While he was doing that Perkins pulled her phone off of her hip and called the plate number in.

Peterson found that all of the doors were locked, so he went over and stood by Perkins waiting for the plate to come back. A gust of wind blew again and he quickly put the cloth back up to his face.

When Perkins got the word back about who the car belonged to, she closed her phone and put it back on her hip.

She looked up at Peterson and said, "Well, at least this time I don't have to make two calls. The car is already impounded so all I have to do is call for forensics. This is the missing woman's car." Peterson did not want to stay in the impound lot and let the dust keep triggering his allergies. He removed the cloth from his face and told Perkins, "If I don't get out of here soon, you are going to have to call forensics for me."

"We don't want that, let's go wait in the car." she told him. They told the worker that they were going to go and wait in the car until someone from the crime scene unit arrived. They went back out to their car and while sitting in it Peterson told Perkins, "We might as well kill two birds with one stone. You can call the number that you have for Chambers and see if he will let us stop by after we leave here to interview him."

Perkins pulled out her pad and flipped it open to the page that had Helen Morgan at the top. She pulled her phone back off of her hip and dialed the number for Gary Chambers. He answered on the second ring and Perkins advised him as to why she was calling. She asked him if it would be possible for her and her partner to come and interview him. He told her that he would be at home until he left for work, which would be at ten o'clock."

Perkins informed him that they would be there before he left for work. She also told him that she would give him a call, when they were on their way. He replied that he would be waiting for their call. Perkins ended the call and put the phone back on her hip.

They sat in the car for twenty minutes before someone from the forensics scene showed up to dust for prints. When the technician was finished, Peterson and Perkins got back into their car and headed to Gary Chambers residence.

13

James had left work early, so that he could go home and confront Jerry. Because James was so nervous, he drove erratically all the way home. He was lucky that he did not get pulled over by the police. He could not stay inside of the yellow lines and he shifted back and forth from lane to lane on the freeway without using the proper signals. He also drove way over the speed limit in his hurry to get home.

When he pulled into the driveway of their home, he shut the car off and quickly got out of it. He rushed up onto the porch, unlocked the door and stormed inside of the house. Soon as he entered he started calling Jerry's name loudly, "Jerry, where are you? Come show your face now!"

He stood in the middle of the living room, waiting for Jerry to answer him. When he got no response he figured that there was only one place that he could be. He went to the door that led down into the basement. He opened it then descended the stairs. When James got down there, he went over to the storage closet that Jerry had converted into an office. He snatched the door opened and found Jerry inside.

James spoke to him, "I know you heard me calling your name?"

"Yea, I heard you James, but there was no need for me to answer you. I knew that you would eventually find me. Now that you have found me, please tell me why you were making all that commotion?"

"I'll tell you what it was for. The police have found that woman and they are investigating her death. Her murder has been all over the news!"

"Okay, so what is the problem James?"

"What's the problem? The problem is they may link her killing to us."

"And how do you suppose they are going to do that?"

"Hell, I don't know, it could be through forensics or technology."

"We have nothing to worry about. You are getting yourself all worked up for nothing."

"Jerry, you are too smart for your own good. Your abnormal behavior is going to bring us both down. It is time for me to put my foot down before I let you destroy us both. I'm not asking you this time, I am telling you to stop this madness. I don't want you kidnapping or hurting anymore women. It doesn't matter if they are weak or not. You're not God and he hasn't given you the authority to pass judgment on them. And he sure did not give you the authority to inflict punishment on them."

"I have never seen you this way James. All this time, I have been questioning if you have any balls or not. You couldn't stand up to the weak women that caused you pain, yet you try to stand up to me. You are lucky that I don't strap you down and make you one of my patients. I'll tell you what I will do for you though. I promise you that I won't harm anyone else until after this thing with that woman blows over."

James knew that he could not really stop Jerry's madness or control him. He knew that he was going to have to accept Jerry's compromise or he wouldn't get anything from him.

"So, you are promising me that you are not going to hurt anyone, while the police are searching for that woman's killer?"

"You have my word James." All James could do, was hope that Jerry kept his word. He emerged from the basement, made him a glass of water then headed up to his bedroom. When he entered his bedroom, he sat on his bed and removed the bottle of valiums from his pocket. He took two of the pills, washed them down with the glass of water then he reached over and placed the glass on the nightstand.

Afterwards, he laid down thinking that after he got some rest he might wake up feeling better.

λ

Peterson and Perkins arrived at the home of Gary Chambers. When they pulled to the curb in front of his residence, they found him to be standing on his porch. He stood there waiting for their arrival. The detectives got out of their car and approached the house. When they got to the bottom of the steps, Peterson looked up and asked the man, "Mr. Chambers."

"Yes, this is me detective, come on up into the house." Chambers turned and headed inside of his house and Peterson and Perkins climbed the stairs. Chambers stood holding the screen door open so that the detectives could enter. Perkins took in the fact, that Chambers had an easygoing attitude. She also took in his sharp features, his bleached blond hair and his steel grey eyes. To her Chambers should have been an actor instead of a cashier.

Once they were in the house, Chambers led them into the living room and told them, "Please have a seat detectives." Peterson and Perkins took a seat on a couch next to each other. Then Chambers asked them, "Can I get you anything to drink?" Both of the detectives declined his offer, so he took a seat in an arm chair that sat facing the couch. When he sat down he turned his attention to Perkins and said, "So detective on the phone you said that you are investigating the disappearance of a woman?"

"Yes we are and we believe that whatever happened to her took place in the parking lot of the store that you work at."

"When did it take place?"

"It was two nights ago."

"I was working the night shift two nights ago."

Peterson finally spoke, "We would like for you to take a look at this picture," he said to him as he removed the photo from his pocket. Chambers got out of his chair and walked over and took the picture from Peterson's outstretched hand.

He looked at the picture and instantly recognized the woman.

"Yeah, she was in the store the other night. I see her in the store at least once a week. She came into the store about one or one thirty in the morning the other night." Peterson's antennas went up. From the information that Chambers had just provided, he knew that the lady had to come up missing while leaving the store on her way to her car.

He asked Chambers, "Was there anybody with her when she was in the store?"

"She was inside by herself, but there was a man in line behind her, trying to make nice with her. I remember he offered to carry one of her bags and she had accepted."

"What did the guy look like?"

"I'm not good with details, but I know that he was a white male and he stood at least six feet tall."

"What about the color of his hair, or his eyes?"

"As I said, I'm not very good with details and I did not pay too much attention to him."

"My guess is a market as big as Kroger's has to be equipped with cameras."

"Yes, the store does have cameras. You would have to see the manager to view any video footage."

"Okay, Mr. Chambers, thank you for your time and help." Peterson told him as him and Perkins rose up off of the couch.

"No problem detective." Chambers replied as he escorted them to the door. When they got back into their car, Peterson said to Perkins, "Well back to Kroger's we go." Peterson was intent on cracking the case. He felt that as long as they did not find another body, then there was still a chance that the missing woman was still alive.

Perkins admired Peterson's persistence. She knew that, once he set his mind on doing something that he wasn't stopping until he completed the task. Because of his determination and persistence, there was no doubt in her mind that they would find out what happened to the missing woman. She pulled out her pad and started going over her notes as Peterson drove.

14

Peterson and Perkins arrived back at the store. When they entered, they found that the shift had changed and a different cashier was working the counter.

They approached the counter and Peterson spoke to the cashier, "I'm detective Peterson and I would like to see the manager Mr. McGee." The cashier responded, "Hold on, I will page him." She picked up the phone and called to the manager's office and told him that there were two detectives at her checkout counter. She hung up the phone then said to the detectives, "He said he is on his way." They stood there until the manager arrived. When he approached them they noticed that he had a jacket on and briefcase in his hand.

When he got to them he asked them, "Did you find the car?"

"Yes, we found it and once again thanks for your help."

"I was just about to head out of here, but I know the two of you did not just drive out here to tell me thanks again. What can I help you guys with now?"

"We visited Gary Chambers and he confirmed that the missing woman was in fact in here the night that she disappeared. He also informed us that there was a man in line behind her, who offered to carry her bags and she accepted. We need to see video footage from all the cameras that you have in the store so that we can identify the man."

"Sure detective, there is no one waiting on me at home anyway." he said to them and smiled. He told them,

"Follow me," then he led the way to the back of the store, then up a flight of steps that led to the security room.

The manager knocked on the door and a man that was dressed in a security guard uniform opened it. The manager spoke to the guard, "Al, I need you to rewind the cameras back two nights ago for these detectives. They are looking for a man who might have kidnapped a woman out in the parking lot."

The security guard looked at the detectives and said, "Come on in, I will do what I can to help you." Peterson and Perkins stepped into the office with the manager pulling up the rear. The security guard sat down at the controls of the security system. There were ten monitor screens that received video feed from twenty cameras.

"When the guard was seated at the controls he asked the detectives, "You say that it was two nights ago?"

"Yes it was," replied Peterson.

"Well you are lucky that only forty eight hours have elapsed. This system continuously records and it uses the same film over. After seventy two hours, the system starts recording new footage over the old footage. I been telling management that they need to upgrade this security system but since we are way out here in the boondocks they don't too much worry about crime. Let me see what I can do for you." He told them as he started hitting buttons on the control panel.

"Two nights ago would have been the 23rd. What time are you looking for?" he asked them.

"Between one and one thirty." Peterson responded. The guard hit some more buttons and all of the monitors started showing video feed that they had received two nights ago. Each monitor was showing different parts of the store. When the security guard had all of the feeds set at one o'clock he hit play and the time at the bottom of the screen started moving. Peterson took in how fussy the monitors were. They did not give you a clear view of any part of the store.

"Is this the clearest that you can get the video to show?" Peterson asked the guard.

"It doesn't get any clearer than this. Like I told you this is an old system and the owner has been too cheap to upgrade it."

"Watch what you say Al, or I will have to report you for insubordination!" The manager told him then laughed.

"This might help you detective." the guard told him. He showed the detectives the sequence of the cameras. He let them know where each monitor was receiving its feed from and that was a big help to them. Peterson first watched the screen that covered the door. At 1:06am, He watched a woman who he thought could be Helen Morgan walk through the door. Because of the whiteness and the fuzziness of the monitor, he could not tell 100% that it was her.

He watched the woman pull a shopping cart out and head down an aisle. Peterson lost visual contact on her for a minute. He started looking at the other monitors until he found her. He kept his attention on the woman as she shopped and every time he lost his visual on her he started looking at the other screens until he located her.

He was so focused on her that that he did not even notice the man that walked into the store at 1:15am. Luckily Perkins was also watching the monitors. When she saw the man enter the store she called out to Peterson, "Look at this." Peterson turned his attention to the monitor that covered the entrance. He saw what appeared to be a white male had just walked through the doors. Even though he could not get a good look at the man's face, his movements seemed strange to Perkins.

He watched as the man walked through the store as if he wasn't there to shop. He took in the fact that the man did not pull a shopping cart, nor did he walk through the store as if he was shopping.

He lost visual of the man for a moment and when he got the visual back, he saw that the man was in the same aisle as the woman. It was apparent that the man was stalking her. He watched as the man trailed the woman everywhere she went, hanging back just enough so that she wouldn't notice him.

In one aisle, he watched the man pick up an item off of a shelf. The man put the item under his arm then pulled something out of his back pocket. Peterson turned his attention to the woman and seen that she had left the aisle.

He quickly turned to look at the other monitors and found that she was heading to the checkout counter. He turned back to the other monitor, just in time to see the man heading out of it. Perkins told the security guard to freeze monitor two and rewind monitor four back thirty seconds. When he did, Peterson looked up from the screen and said, "Why did you do that?"

"I want you to see something, watch this," she told him then she told the guard, "Hit play for camera four." The guard hit the play button and together they watched the man pull something out of his inside jacket pocket, screwed what looked to be a top off and poured something into whatever it was that he held in his hand. They watched as he put the top back on what they believed to be a bottle and put it back inside of his jacket pocket. They saw him fold whatever it was he had in his hand and put it in his back pocket then they watched him leave the aisle.

Peterson could not believe that he had missed that. He thought to himself how sometimes he did not know what he would do without Perkins. Perkins told the guard, "Now hit play for monitor two." The guard did and they watched the man get into line behind the woman and strike up a conversation with her. They watched as the woman stood and waited on the man after her bags had been filled, then they watched the man lift one of her bags and together they headed out of the store.

Peterson asked the guard, "What about the cameras on the outside of the store?"

"I'll see what I can do." the guard told him then started hitting buttons on the control panel. Two of the monitors started showing the parking lot. Peterson seen that the screen was almost pitch black. It was as if there was no lighting at all in the parking lot.

The security guard still rewound the film back, to the date and time that he had rewound the inside cameras to. Seconds after the inside monitors had showed the two people leaving the store, the camera outside of the store showed two shadows walking through the parking lot. When they reached a certain point, the shadows disappeared completely. Peterson found himself becoming frustrated. He felt that they were so close to solving the case. He was upset by the fact that a cheap surveillance system was preventing him from solving the case.

He thought for a minute, trying to figure out what else could be done. Perkins seen his frustration and spoke out, "We can have forensics take a look at the film. They may be able to enhance the images and give us a clearer picture of the man and woman on the film."

Perkins took in what she had just said then a smile appeared on his face. "He said to Perkins, "You're amazing, I could kiss you right now."

"You do and I will have you brought up on charges for sexual harassment." she replied with a smile on her face.

Peterson asked the manager, "Is it a way that we can get copies of the video footage showing the man and woman inside and outside of the store?" The manager directed Peterson's question to the security guard, "Can it be done Al?"

"It can be done, but unfortunately there is no disc to burn them on. All the footage is on the hard drive, if I had a disc I could burn a copy for you."

"Shit!" Peterson said loudly. Perkins looked at him and he said, "Excuse my French." The security guard still wanting to be of assistance, quickly thought of an alternative, he looked up at Peterson and said, "If Mr. McGhee would approve it and if you give me an email address, I could send you a copy of the footage as an email attachment."

Peterson turned his attention on the store man-ager, who quickly stated, "Do whatever you can to help them Al."

"All I need is an email address?" Perkins pulled out a pad and pen and wrote down her email address at the Cleveland police department. She handed the paper to the guard and he told them, "By the time you guys get to the station, the footage will be at that email address you gave me."

Peterson thanked the guard, then for the third time that day he thanked the manager. The manager left out of the security booth with the detectives and they all headed for the store's exit. Once outside the manager shook hands with both detectives, then they went their separate ways.

λ

Peterson and Perkins got back into their car and headed back to the station. They had been in the field for over 12 hours and they both felt drained.

Peterson had one more thing that he wanted to take care of before he called it a night. When they got to the station he had Perkins pull up the footage and burn it onto a disk. He put the disk in the top drawer of his desk then locked his desk. He did not want anything to happen to it before he had a chance, to get forensics to look at it.

15

Jerry crept upstairs to James' room. He walked quietly to prevent from waking him. When he got to James' room, he carefully turned the doorknob and pushed the door open.

He stuck his head inside of the door and saw James' sleeping figure in the bed. He pushed the door further open and stepped inside. Once inside the room he stood still for a few minutes, listening to James' labored breathing. When he was satisfied that James was truly sound asleep and would not wake up, he crept over to the night stand and removed James' car keys.

After getting the keys, Jerry retraced his steps, creeping back out of the room. He went back down the stairs and headed out of the house.

Even though Jerry had promised James that he wouldn't harm any women until things blew over with the woman he had kidnapped from the hospital, he found that he had an overwhelming urge to find a patient.

Jerry gave into that urge not even 24 hours after he had made the promise to James. He figured that what James did not know would not hurt him.

It was almost one in the morning and Jerry knew that it was only a few places to find a patient at that time of night. He got into the car, started it, and then pulled out of the driveway. His destination was West 40th and Detroit. He knew that on Cleveland's lower west side, prostitutes strolled up and down the street trying to solicit Johns.

Jerry wanted to get a patient and be done with them before James woke up. He knew that time was limited. He had five hours at max, to get a patient, perform surgery on them, then dispose of the body.

He intended to get a hooker inside of the car and use chloroform on her to subdue her. He had a chloroformed soaked handkerchief in his inside jacket pocket.

As soon as Jerry reached West 40th and Detroit, he saw numerous prostitutes on both sides of the street. He also heard the whistles and cat calls they gave him as the Cadillac Seville drove slowly down the street.

Jerry slowed the car almost to a complete stop as he looked over the hookers as he drove. Some of the women stepped off the curb and modeled for him, trying to get him to select them.

"Hey honey," one said trying to flag him down. Jerry kept going and up ahead he spotted a tall blond woman with huge breast standing at the curb.

Jerry had no time to figure out why he had a thing for blond women with big tits. He pulled to a stop in front of the woman and rolled his passenger's side window down. The hooker walked up to his car and leaned inside of his window, "You looking for a date?" she asked him.

"How much?" Jerry asked her.

"It depends on what you want. For oral sex its seventy five dollars. For a little honey it's a hundred and fifty, but for you sugar I will give you special treatment for one fifty."

"What does the special treatment entail?"

"It entails all of me. I will give you my all."

"I'll take that," Jerry told her with a smile on his face. He hit the door locks unlocking the passenger's door.

The hooker climbed into the car and asked him, "Do you want to get a room or do it in here?"

"We don't need a room for what we are about to do sweetheart." Jerry told the hooker.

Jerry did not want to leave any evidence and he knew that checking into a motel would leave a paper trail. Plus he did not want any witnesses to be able to point him out.

The prostitute told him, "Pull down to that stop sign and make a right." Jerry did as he was told and when he got halfway down the street, she directed him to turn down an alley that was a dead end. Jerry pulled all the way to the dead end.

The prostitute lifted up the armrest that separated them and put her hands into his lap. She unzipped his pants, reached inside and pulled his penis out of his boxers. She freed his penis and started stroking it, Jerry took in a deep breath and he found himself getting aroused.

The prostitute liked to encourage her customers in hopes that she could keep them coming back. She also knew that when you stroked their egos they gave you nice tips. When Jerry's penis was fully erect in her hands, it was no more than four or five inches long, but she looked in his eyes and said, "I see you are a big boy. I know you're gonna fill momma up."

Jerry knew that she was lying, but it did not matter to him. He knew that the punishment that he was going to inflict on her would cover her lies.

The hooker lowered her head and took him into her mouth. A feeling of pleasure swept over Jerry. The feeling was so intense that he decided to let her finish before he incapacitated her.

He closed his eyes to enjoy the feeling, and then abruptly the feeling of pleasure went away. He opened his eyes and looked down and saw that the hooker had removed herself from him. While still breathing hard he asked her, "Why did you stop?"

"Because you get half and half sugar. You just experienced the first half, and now it's time for the second half." The prostitute lifted her skirt up showing her hairy bush. Jerry took in the fact that her pubic hairs were a different color than the hair on top of her head. He found himself getting angry because she wasn't naturally blond. He felt the urge to use violence on her right there, but he knew if he did things would never go as planned. He decided that he would give her extra punishment when they got to his office.

He told the hooker, "It would be more comfortable if we got into the back seat."

"We can get back there, but just remember sugar, that this money for sex and time is money. So if you try to make love to me, I'm going to have to charge you more." After she finished her statement she opened the car door and got out. She shut the front door then opened the back door. She lifted her skirt then sat down and scooted back.

Jerry got out of the car and pulled the soaked cloth out of his pocket. He walked around to the passenger's side with his penis still hanging out the front of his pants. When he got to the back door, the hooker raised her legs and pulled them back, inviting Jerry inside of her.

Jerry climbed into the car and the hooker reached out and grabbed a hold of his penis. She guided him inside of her as he lowered himself down on her.

When Jerry had lowered himself all the way down, he raised his left hand and brought it down over the woman's nose and mouth. The woman's eyes became as large as saucers and she tried to raise her arms in order to force him off, but before she had a chance to react, she was unconscious.

The act of what Jerry was doing had caused him to become aroused again and he knew that the woman could not cut his pleasure short for a second time. He stroked himself inside of the woman no more than three times and started to release himself inside of her.

Once he had emptied himself, he stood up and straightened himself out. He lifted the woman's limp legs and pushed her completely inside of the car. He shut the door, then hurried around and jumped back inside of the car.

He pulled out of the alley and headed home and while he was driving he hummed his favorite song to himself. When he got to the house, he shut the car off and got out of it and opened the back door. He pulled the woman from the car, picked her up and laid her over his shoulder. He shut the car door, and then headed up the steps. He opened the door, carried her into the house and down into his office.

16

Jerry took the unconscious woman over to one of the cubicles, slid the plastic curtain open and laid her on the operating table. He removed all of the woman's clothing, and then secured her body with leather restraints. He used a leather strap to pin her head down and covered her mouth with a strip of adhesive tape, so that no one would be able to hear her screams.

Once he had her secure, he got two trays that held his operating equipment and positioned them next to the operating table. One tray held surgical tools and the other held carpentry tools.

After he had everything in place, he went to his change room to put on his operating gear. He put on a one piece plastic jumpsuit, plastic footies and latex gloves.

He did that so that, he wouldn't leave any DNA. He stepped out of the change room and approached the cubicle that the woman was in, humming his favorite tune.

When he entered the cubicle he found that his patient was awake. She heard him enter the cubicle and tried to turn her head, only to find that the strap prevented her from doing so. She had to wait until Jerry walked over to the table to see him.

Jerry looked down at the woman and saw in her eyes that she was terrified. To Jerry that only confirmed what he had been trying to get James to see for the longest, that women were weak. Jerry spoke to the woman, "Everything is going to be alright. After I perform surgery on you there will be no more pain. You will no longer have to sale your soul to live in this ugly world." The woman knew from the words he spoke that he intended to hurt her.

Tears started falling from her eyes and rolling down her cheeks. She looked at Jerry with pleading eyes and that only upset him. Jerry screamed at the woman, "You stop that! Stop it now!"

The woman looking at him with that look in her eyes made him feel emotionally and mentally conflicted. It tugs at his conscious, because in his subconscious he knew that what he was doing was wrong.

Jerry thought to himself that he had no intentions of becoming weak like James. In his mind he knew what he had to do, so that he could finish the operation without interruption.

He reached over to the table that contained the surgical tools and picked up a scalpel. He went to the end of the table and stood behind her head. Then he leaned over her and used his thumb and index finger on his left hand to hold her left eye lid open. Even though she was strapped to the table, the woman tried to twist and turn and shake herself loose.

The strap around her head kept her head secured as Jerry brought his right hand down steadily. He used the surgical knife to make an incision at the bottom of her eye socket. The knife easily cut through the soft tissue and Jerry made a complete circle around her eye socket.

When he was done, he used the tip of the scalpel to remove the circle of skin. Blood ran down the woman's face and her eyes rapidly shifted back and forth from left to right. She could not communicate the pain that she was feeling through sound, but her contorted facial expressions gave an indication of the type of pain that she was in.

Jerry bought the knife back down and started cutting through the tendons and eye muscles and because of their toughness, he had to use a little more force than he used with the skin. When he completed the circle, he again used the tip of the knife only this time he used it to pop her eyeball out of its socket.

The woman's eyeball popped up in the air and Jerry caught it in his left hand. He sat the eye on the tray, and then proceeded to use the same procedure on the woman's right eye.

The woman went into shock while he was re-moving her other eye and she passed out. Once he completed his task, Jerry said to himself, "Anything that brings you weakness you have to cast out. Now I can begin the operation."

He turned to the table that held the carpenter's tools, and picked up a power saw. He used the power saw to remove all of the woman's limbs. After removing two of them, her breathing became erratic, and Jerry knew that she did not have much time left.

To keep her from bleeding out, he used a small torch to sear the area from which the limb had been removed. The smell of the torch combined with the smell of burning flesh was enough to make any human being feel nauseated.

The smell of the burning flesh only aroused Jerry. By the time he removed her other two limbs and seared the places where they had been removed from the woman was barely breathing. To end it all, he performed the last part of the surgery, by severing her head.

Even though Jerry had cut every limb from her body, the limbs were still secured by the restraints. He went and retrieved four hefty two-ply trash bags and doubled them up. He unsecured the woman's limbs and placed them inside of one of the bags. When he unsecured the woman's head it rolled off the table, falling onto the floor. Jerry picked it up and placed it into the bag with her limbs, and then he used a tie to secure the bag.

He then lifted the woman's torso off the table and placed it in the other bag by itself. He did the same thing he did with the first bag, used a tie to secure the bag.

Afterwards, he went and turned on a power hose that was connected to a container filled with water and bleach. He knew that water and bleach would mix in with the blood and dilute it, which would make it easy to wash away.

He sprayed the whole cubicle, even the operating table. He used the pressure from the hose to push the diluted blood down the drain that was in the middle of the floor.

When he was done he went back into the change room and took off the plastic outfit and footies, all of which he was going to burn.

He looked at his watch, seen that it was 3:45am and smiled to himself. He knew that he still had time to give before James would awake. He went over and picked up the garbage bags and carried them up the steps. He took them out of the house and placed them in the trunk of the car. He got into the car and drove to the same industrial area that he went to dispose of the last body. He drove down to the flats, where there were many factories.

He pulled into the parking lot of a factory that made vacuum cleaners and pulled next to a commercial dumpster that sat at the back of the parking lot. He took one of the bags out of the trunk and put it in the dumpster. He got back into the car, pulled out of the factory's lot and drove for a short distance before he pulled into the lot of another factory. He pulled up to the dumpster that was on their property and put the other bag into it.

Done with everything, he got back into the car and headed home. He hummed his favorite song all the way there. Once he got home, he took the plastic clothing out back and burned it until it was just a clump of molt. He then went back into the house, showered and went to bed. He was sound asleep by the time James woke up.

17

The next day, Peterson came into work early because he wanted to get somebody from forensics to look at the video feed that was on the disk.

He knew that he was going against policy, be-cause he was cutting through red tape. He was about to ask forensics to set aside things that had already been submitted for testing to review the footage. Luckily for him he had someone in forensics who owed him a favor and he intended to call that favor in.

Sitting at his desk, he called the extension for Samantha Stevens at the crime scene investigation unit.

She answered her phone, "CSI unit,"

"Samantha, this is Peterson, how is it going?"

"Let's cut the small talk Peterson. You only call when you need a favor. I know that you are one up on me, so what do you need?"

"Damn Sam! You don't have to be so harsh. I thought we were friends?"

"Once again, what do you need Peterson?"

"Okay, Okay, I need you to look at some foot-age that I have on a disk. The footage was recorded by a cheap security system and it has poor quality. I want you to look at it and see if you can enhance the images on it. What's on it is detrimental to solving the case of a missing woman."

"I'm very backed up Peterson. It will be a week be-fore I will be able to get to it."

"The person may be dead by then. The woman is the second of two that disappeared on the same day. The other one was found dead in a ditch on the side of the freeway. I'm trying my best to save this woman before she ends up being found the same way."

"Alright! Alright! But it's still going to take a day before I can get to it."

"I'll take that and thanks Sam."

"Whatever Peterson," she responded then hung up.

Peterson sat there with a shocked expression on his face. He was trying to figure out why Stevens had reacted that way towards him. While he was sitting there, the phone rang and he picked it up. He found that it was Cody Miller calling for the third time in as many days. He understood Miller's urgency and concern relating to his missing fiancé.

Even though Peterson knew that there was a high probability that the woman found on the side of the freeway was his fiancée he knew that he could not tell him. By policy, he had to wait for the DNA results to come back, before he could tell him that his fiancé had been found slain.

Peterson tried to show consideration, "Mr. Miller how are you?"

"I'm not doing too good detective. Have you found out anything yet?"

"We are following up on leads Mr. Miller and as I told you yesterday as soon as I learn something you will be informed."

"What kind of leads are you following up on detective?"

"I'm not at liberty to discuss that with you right now, but soon as I gather some concrete facts, I will be sure to notify you."

"Well detective, Mary's parents are flying in today and I don't think they will be as understanding as I am. They are going to want answers that I can't give them."

"As of right now, I won't be able to tell them anymore than I have already told you. If it would satisfy them, I have no problem telling them the exact same thing that I have told you. If they don't feel comfortable talking to me over the phone, you can bring them down here to talk to me face to face."

"That's just what I think I'll do detective." Cody told him then slammed the phone down in his ear. Peterson heard the dial tone in his ear and pulled the phone away from it. He sat staring at the phone as if he could not believe what had just happened.

Perkins walked into the cubicle while he was sitting there looking at the phone. He saw her come in and hung the phone up. She sat down at her desk then looked over at him.

"What's wrong Pete? You look like you just lost your best friend."

Instead of telling her what he was really thinking about he said, "Have you ever thought about how life is nothing but one big obstacle course?"

"What do you mean by that?"

"I mean every time you get past one obstacle you're sure to run right into another one. It never stops as long as you're breathing?"

"I see what you're saying, but you can't ever let that get you down. Just stay ready and prepared to knock down each one that pops up."

"I like your insight Perkins." he told her just as his phone started ringing. He picked it up and listened for about three minutes, then he hung up and said to Perkins, "Well another one just popped up."

"You mean an obstacle?"

"No a woman's dead body, no scratch that, parts of a woman's dead body. Recycling workers at the garbage recycling plant found all of a woman's limbs along with an eyeless head inside of a garbage bag."

"You can't be serious?"

"I'm serious as the air we breathe."

"What about the rest of the body, have they found it?"

"They are scouring through the trash right now looking for the torso. Hopefully they will find it before we get there."

Peterson took the disk out of his desk drawer, put it in his pocket then said to Perkins, "Come on, we have to make a stop down at headquarters to drop this disk off at forensics, then we have to head over to the plant."

Together they left the station, got into their car and headed downtown to the Cleveland police headquarters.

When they got down there, Perkins sat in the car going over her notes while Peterson went inside and caught the elevator up to the 4th floor.

He got off the elevator and walked to the crime scene investigation unit. He told the lady at the front desk that he was there to see Samantha Stevens and she notified Sam that he was up front.

Sam appeared at the front desk in less than a minute. Peterson knew from the look on her face that she still had an attitude with him for some reason. He thought to himself when he had time, he was going to try and figure out what he had done to her. He had no clue as to why she seemed to be upset with him.

He gave her the disk and with a smirk on her face she told him, "As soon as I see if I can enhance the images enough to be of any help, I will contact you." Peterson thanked her again, and then headed back out to the car. He got in the car and drove over to the city's west side.

When they pulled into the lot of the plant it was like dejavu. The lot was filled with reporters from every news station in Cleveland, "How do they do that?" Peterson asked Perkins.

"How do they do what?"

"How do they know what's going on before we do. You would think the police are supposed to be the first on the scene, but somehow the media is always at the crime scene before we get there."

"I can't give you the answer to that." she told him as he parked the car. Soon as they were out of the car, the reporters flocked to them. Peterson wondered if it was strictly a coincidence that the same reporter from the scene where the woman was found by the freeway was there.

Just like Peterson remembered the reporter, the reporter remembered him also. He was the first to stick a mic in Peterson's face and ask, "Detective have you reached a different conclusion, than the one you had three days ago now that another body has been found?"

"No, I have not reached a different conclusion. This investigation has just started and there has been nothing found that would insinuate that this incident is connected to the other. If we do find a link in the future, you will be the first to know. Now if you don't mind, please allow us to do our job." With that being said, Peterson pushed his way through the crowd of reporters, with Perkins right on his heels.

They were met by a uniform officer at the plant's door, who led them into the plant. When they entered the building, both Peterson and Perkins were overcome by the awful smell that deluged the plant.

The plant was split in two parts, one of which was a dump and the other being a recycling plant. The officer escorted them to the part that was the garbage dump. As they got closer the smell almost became unbearable. Peterson pulled a handkerchief out of his pocket and covered his nose with it. Perkins used her jacket collar to cover her nose and mouth.

When they got there Peterson and Perkins had seen numerous law enforcement personnel on the scene. They all had paper masks over their noses, to deal with the smell. Most of them were in the dump, picking through the trash.

Peterson saw two GST investigators standing by an oddly shaped, large garbage bag. One of the forensics guys recognized Peterson and called him over. He and Perkins walked over to the man and when they got to him, he handed them both a paper mask to put on.

Talking through the mask Peterson asked him, "What do you guys have so far Norman?"

"Well, so far all we have is what's in that bag, which is two arms, two legs and a head with no eyes in it."

"What kind of sicko are we dealing with?" asked Peterson.

"It looks like a very sick one Pete."

"Have they found the torso yet?"

"As of now no, they have been picking through the trash for over two hours, but haven't found anything."

Peterson looked out into the dump and knew that it was going to take days upon days to dig through all of the trash that was piled up inside of the dump.

The man from forensics continued, "We took prints from both hands, because there is no way to tell that all the body parts came from the same body. We are going to have to take the head in to try and compare the teeth with dental records."

Peterson pulled out the picture of Helen Morgan then said, "Norman is it possible for me to take a look at the head?"

"Sure, if you can stomach it, I have no problem with it." Norman opened the bag, then reached inside and pulled the head out. With both of his hands on the sides of the severed head, he held it up for Peterson to look at it.

Perkins cringed as she looked at the severed head, with an eyeless face. Peterson looked at the face of the eyeless head, then to the picture that he held in his hand. Even with the eyes being removed, Peterson could still tell by the hair and the facial features that the head was that of Helen Morgan.

Peterson knew that he would have to notify her next of kin and have them make a positive identification. He could not phantom the idea of having them identify the woman from looking at something as grotesque as an eyeless severed head.

Peterson thought to himself that there had to be another way in which the family could identify the woman. An idea appeared in his head and he asked the man from forensics, "Norman, is there any distinguishing marks on any of the body parts such as tattoos or piercings, or maybe any jewelry?"

Norman thought for a minute and then said, "You know what, and there is a class ring on the ring finger of the left hand."

"Could I see it?" Peterson asked him.

"Sure," he responded, then went back inside the bag and pulled an arm out. He seen that it was the wrong one, so he put it back in there and pulled the other arm out. Peterson could see the class ring on her finger. He knelt down to take a closer look at the ring and seen that it had a green emerald inside of it. On the side of the ring there was an engraving and Peterson read it out loud, "Class of 2008."

He wanted to know what was on the inside of the ring. He asked Norman, "Can you remove it, so I can see if there is any inscription on the inside."

"If that's what you want, sure." he responded then twisted the ring off the woman's finger. Peterson reached inside of his pocket and found that he did not have any more latex gloves. Norman knew what he was looking for when he dug into his pocket, so he dug into his own and pulled out an extra pair. He handed them to Peterson, who put them on then took a hold of the ring.

He examined the inside of the ring, but was disappointed when he did not find an inscription inside. He figured that he had a better chance of seeing if the woman's mother could identify the ring. He told Norman, "I need to hold on to this. I will enter it into evidence after I see if it can help me with finding out the woman's identity."

"Suit yourself put it in here." he told him then handed him a plastic baggie. Peterson took the baggie placed the ring inside of it, then turned to Perkins and said, "There is nothing more that we can do here. I say we go visit Helen Morgan's mother and see if she can identify this ring."

"I second that motion, lead the way boss," she said with a smile on her face. Soon as they stepped outside of the plant, they removed the paper masks and took in deep breaths.

"I never knew the true value of fresh air until I walked inside of that plant." Peterson said to Perkins as they walked down the steps of the plant.

They headed towards their car only to get swarmed by the reporters again. Peterson seen that the same reporter was at the front of the pack and said to himself, "He's a persistent little rascal." The reporter stuck his mic out and asked him, "Is it true that only the dead woman's limbs and an eyeless head was found?"

"All I will tell you is that we are looking for one sick individual. Give me a close up with your camera." The reporter told his cameraman to get a close up and when he got in position Peterson looked straight into the camera and said, "As I said whoever did this is one sick individual and whoever you are, just know that your days are numbered. I will find you and I'm going to bring you to justice."

Peterson turned and walked away from the reporters with Perkins at his side. The reporters followed them trying to get more comments out of them, but the two detectives ignored them as they walked to their car, got in and pulled off heading to the home of Helen Morgan.

18

James was sitting in the hospital's break room, taking his lunch break. He sat sipping a cup of coffee, while he watched the mid-morning news.

Ever since he had seen the news clipping about the woman that was found on the side of the freeway, he watched the news every chance he got. He wanted to stay abreast of any new developments in the case. The news went to a commercial break and James started drifting into deep thought.

He started thinking about the advanced methods the police used in tracking down criminals. James was a doctor and he knew how advanced technology had become. He knew that the tiniest piece of fiber or a single strand of hair could disclose the identification of a criminal. He thought to himself, "Jerry is not a real doctor, so he doesn't understand these things."

James felt that it was his job to protect him and Jerry both. He felt that if Jerry went down that he would be taken down also. James sat there thinking how ironic it was that he was a doctor yet had an uncanny relationship with a killer. He rationalized to himself that the world was filled with contradiction. He was just glad that Jerry had given him his word that he was going to stop his devilish activities, at least for the time being.

The commercials ended and the news came back on. Soon as it came back on the anchorman said, "Now for today's breaking news. Today authorities were called to the city's garbage recycling plant to investigate one of the most gruesome crimes that this city has seen in years."

The anchorman's words caught James' attention and he sat up with his eyes glued to the TV screen.

The anchorman continued, "Workers at the plant found a garbage bag that was filled with human body parts." Hearing that, James thought he was about to pass out. He started hyper ventilating, his heart rate went up and he started to feel dizzy. He was so caught up that he did not even here Rebecca calling his name. She had to call his name three times before he finally noticed her. He finally looked up and seen her standing there holding a food tray.

She asked him, "What's on your mind? I had to call your name three times."

"I'm just watching the mid-morning news." he told her then turned his attention back to the television. Rebecca without an invitation took a seat at the table with him. She had seen how engrossed he was in the TV, so she began eating her food, while looking at him.

Rebecca found that no matter how many times she saw James, she found herself mesmerized by his distinguishing looks. Staring at his face she noticed that he had two healing scars on the left side of his face. She thought that his face was too handsome to be having scars on it. She inquired about how he had gotten the scars.

"James how did you manage to get those scars on your face?" James turned towards her for a second and said, "Ah, I cut myself shaving," then he quickly turned his attention back towards the TV. He was caught up in it so much, that Rebecca decided to tune in also. They both sat watching the television and listened as the anchorman mentioned that they were about to go live to a reporter that was at the city's recycling plant.

The screen split and a reporter came onto the screen. The anchorman started asking him questions, "Terry, what happened there?"

"Well Rick, today authorities were called to this recycling plant behind me after workers at the plant made a gruesome find. While sifting through trash in the dump they came upon a garbage bag that was filled with human body parts."

"Terry, I know it's kind of unnerving but could you tell us exactly what body parts were found?"

"Yes, they found the limbs and a head that they think all belong to a woman. Also a source within the police department told us that both eyes had been removed from the head."

"That sounds very disturbing Terry!"

"Yes it does Rick."

"And you said the bag only contained the limbs and a head?"

"Yes,"

"So, no midsection or shall I say, no torso was found?"

"No there wasn't Rick. Several authorities as well as plant workers are cyphering through the city dump trying to locate the torso."

James' body began to tremble when he heard those words and his breathing started to become erratic. He knew that the parts that they found had to belong to the woman that Jerry had taken into the basement. He felt that things were getting out of hand and he knew that if Jerry kept killing that it would only be a matter of time before the police ended up tracking Jerry down. The anchorman asked the reporter, "Terry does the authorities have any clues in the case?"

"As of now they have not been able to do any of the following, they do not have any suspects, they have not determined how the woman was killed and they have yet been able to identify the woman."

"One last question Terry, do the authorities see any connection between this murder and the one where the woman was found slain on the side of the freeway?"

"Authorities say they have found no evidence that would suggest that the two murders are connected."

"Okay thank you Terry, we are about to show the viewers a clip of you interviewing a law enforcement officer earlier."

"I'll see you back at the station Rick." The screen went back to full caption and the anchorman said, "Now we are going to show you a clip that was taken a couple hours ago of our news correspondent interviewing a detective on the case. Listen to what one Cleveland detective had to say about the crime."

The screen split again and a clip of the reporter interviewing the detective appeared on the screen. There was a close up of the detective looking dead into the screen as he spoke, "As I said, whoever committed this crime is one sick individual and whoever you are, I just want you to know that your days are numbered. I will find you and I am going to bring you to justice."

The confidence in the man's voice scared James so much that he shook almost all of his coffee out of the cup, spilling it onto the table and the front of his shirt.

The news clip of the horrible murder had shaken Rebecca and she turned to James to make a comment about the vicious killing. When she turned towards him, she had seen spilled coffee all over the table and on his shirt. She looked up at his face and swore to herself that he looked as if he had just seen a ghost. She asked him, "James are you alright?"

"Uh … Uh … Yes I'm fine." he told her then reached for some napkins to wipe the coffee off the table and to clean the front of his shirt.

"There are some sick people in this world, I hope they catch that sick bastard." she said to James, who did not comment. She asked him, "How could someone do something so horrible?"

"I have no idea." James told her as he stood up.

"Where are you going?"

"I have to make my rounds." he told her, then hurried out of the break room.

James rushed back to his office and called the hospital's administrator. He told the administrator that he had a family emergency and had to leave work immediately. The administrator gave him the okay and James grabbed his briefcase and headed out of the hospital. His destination was home. He had to tell Jerry about the police latest find.

After James left, Rebecca sat there and finished eating her food. As she sat there eating, she wondered why it was that James had been acting strange lately. She couldn't figure out why he acted the way he did while watching the news clip. She liked James a lot, so she tried to rationalize his behavior, by concluding that he still hadn't gotten over his wife leaving him. She got up from the table, dumped her tray, and then headed back to her office.

19

Peterson and Perkins pulled to a stop in front of Helen Morgan's home. They got out of the car and approached the house. Peterson knocked on the door and Helen's mother answered it. Soon as she saw the detectives at her door, she started crying. Just from the serious looks on the detective's faces she knew that something was terribly wrong.

Peterson asked her, "Ms. Morgan would it be alright if we came inside?"

"Please tell me my daughter is okay? Lord, please let them tell me she is alright." Peterson knew that it was going to be harder than he thought to deliver her the bad news. He said to her, "Ms. Morgan, it would be best if we came inside to talk to you."

"Oh God No! She is dead isn't she? I know she's dead!" she screamed then turned and walked away from the door.

Peterson pulled the screen door open and him and Perkins stepped inside the house. They followed Ms. Morgan into the living room where she flopped down onto the couch and began crying all out.

They heard footsteps and turned to the direction that the sounds were coming from. They had seen the woman's two grandchildren running down the stairs. The kids went over to their grandmother and started crying right along with her.

The little boy asked her, "What's wrong granny?" Their grandmother outstretched both of her arms out and pulled the children into an embrace. Through her cries she told them, "It's going to be okay, I'm going to take care of you two." The little girl remembered the detectives. She turned around in her grandmother's arms, looked up at Peterson and asked him, "Did you find my mommy?" Peterson did not even know how to respond to that question. He found himself getting upset.

He was getting upset with whoever it was that had taken the children's mother away from them. He vowed to himself that he was going to find the killer and bring him to justice.

Perkins went over and sat next to the woman and her grandchildren. She knew what the woman was going through. She had felt the same type of emotional pain, when her father killed her mother. She tried to reach out to the woman, "Ms. Morgan I know you hurting right now, but you have to remain strong for your grandchildren. We have something that we need to show you. It will help us in knowing if the person we believe to be your daughter is in fact truly her."

Peterson removed the plastic baggie that held the ring from his pocket and walked over to the woman. She had her head down, still crying when he held his hand out and said, "Ms. Morgan have you ever seen this ring before?" The woman looked up and took the bag out of his hand. She raised it up to her face and examined it closely. When she read the engraving on the side of the ring she fell over onto the floor and started wailing. Her grand kids just stood there crying their little hearts out.

Sometimes Peterson would wonder to himself, why he ever chose to become a homicide detective. He was a man of faith and seeing so much despair, destruction and violence just did not sit well with him.

He had come to the woman's house to do a tough job, but he knew that it had to be done in order to solve the case. He needed to know for a fact if the ring belonged to her daughter. He gently helped her up off the floor and placed her back on the couch, then he asked her again, "Ms. Morgan does that ring belong to your daughter?"

In between her sobs she told him, "Yes, her father bought her that ring for her graduation. Are you sure that she is dead?"

"I'm afraid so, but I promise you that we won't stop until we find her killer."

"When will I be able to see the body?" she asked between sobs.

Peterson did not know how he could explain to her that there wasn't a whole body.

"How can I tell her all we have are her limbs and an eyeless head?" he asked himself. He looked over at Perkins and she hunched her shoulders, indicating that she did not know how to tell the woman either.

Peterson knew that it was up to him. He knew that as a police officer, you had to do whatever needed to be done.

He tried to tell it to her as best he could, "Ms. Morgan, let me start by saying whoever killed your daughter is a very sick individual. It hurts me to have to tell you that your daughter's body wasn't found intact."

"Stop detective! Just stop right there! Now what exactly do you mean, by saying her body was not found intact?"

"It is apparent that whoever killed your daughter, dismembered her and some of her body parts have not been located yet."

"What! Oh God! No! No! No! Who did this to my baby? My only child!" She turned to the detectives and said, "Get out! Get out now! It's your fault for not protecting my baby. It's your fault that she is dead. Get out, I said!"

Peterson and Perkins understood the woman's pain and her irrational thinking. The police were supposed to serve and protect, but usually the police didn't become involved with a crime, until after it was committed.

They turned and walked to the door. They let themselves out, got back into their car and headed back to the station.

While driving, Peterson fell into deep thought. He was thinking that it was time for them to find the evidence that would help them identify there killers. He wanted to bring the sick bastards to justice.

20

When Peterson and Perkins got back to the precinct, they found that things were getting rougher on them by the minute. When they walked through the doors of the precinct they saw that Mary Weathers' whole family was waiting to see them.

Cody Miller was there with his fiancé's parents and her sister. Peterson did not like the fact that Miller pointed him out like he had committed a crime. Soon as he seen Peterson enter the precinct he jumped up, pointed his finger at him and said, "There he is right there!"

Her parents quickly got up off the bench and approached him. Mary's father was the first to speak, "Detective what have you found relating to the disappearance of my daughter." Peterson respected the fact that they were anxious to find their daughter and he decided that it would be best to take them to his desk and explain things to them fully. He asked the father, "Mr. Weathers, I presume?" The man responded angrily, "What does my name have to do with my daughter being missing?"

"Mr. Weathers I understand your frustration and I'm just trying to make the proper acquaintance, so that we can communicate effectively. Now if you don't mind you and your family can follow me to my desk, so that we can discuss this matter."

Mary's father realized that he was directing his anger at the wrong person. He calmed himself down, and then apologized to Peterson, "I apologize detective, and it's just that me and my wife have been blaming ourselves for our daughter's disappearance. If we would have never given in to her and Rachel's pleas to move up here none of this would have happened."

"I accept your apology, now please follow me to my desk." Mary's family followed Peterson and Perkins to their desk. There were only two chairs, so Mary's parents sat down while Mary's sister and fiancé remained standing.

Peterson sat at his desk and got straight to the point, "We are following up on leads regarding Ms. Weathers' disappearance. We are waiting on some solid facts which should be in tomorrow or the day after. What we really do not want to do is jump the gun on things. Just as I informed Mr. Miller, soon as we get some solid facts in the case we will let you know."

"Is it true that her purse was found under her car detective?" Mary's mother asked.

"Yes we did find her purse, and we do think that foul play was involved regarding her disappearance. Give us a day or two and we shall be contacting you."

All while the family was at their desk, Perkins never took her eyes off Cody. Every time Cody looked her way, he found that she was staring at him. Her staring at him like that started to rattle Cody's nerves.

Perkins had drawn her own conclusion. She had run into many criminals that were good actors and to her Cody was one of them. She felt that him being concerned and all up under the missing woman's parents was all a ploy. She thought that instead of him being a concerned fiancé, that he was just a good actor.

After Peterson promised the family that he would be in touch with them in a day or so, the family realized that there was nothing else they could do but wait.

Weather's parents rose out of the chairs and Peterson escorted them up front. Afterwards Peterson went back to his desk, sat down and took a deep breath. He sat there and drifted into deep thought again.

He was thinking about how sometimes his job put a lot of wear and tear on him. He reflected on how his job was a thankless job. Even if he found the killer in a murder and brought him to justice, it was still after the fact. The person who had been killed could not be brought back. Peterson found that he would feel better catching the perp before the act, but he knew that wasn't a reality in his line of work.

Perkins was on her computer filling out her reports, when Peterson snapped out of his thoughts and turned on his computer also. He looked to see if he had any emails but found that he didn't, so he started filling out his daily reports also. When he was finished he felt, drained and couldn't wait to get home and get him a good night's rest. He looked over at Perkins who had just shut her computer off and asked her, "You ready to call it a night?" Perkins looked at her watch then responded, "It looks to be that time."

Peterson shut his computer off, and then together they left the station heading home.

21

Two more days went by before Peterson received any news regarding the murders. That day when he and Perkins got to their desk, he turned his computer on and found that he had over six emails. He had seen that three of those emails were from forensics. He told Perkins, "Today might be our lucky day." then he picked up the phone and called forensics.

The first expert that he talked to was the one assigned to the Weathers' case. The expert explained to Peterson that the DNA results proved that the body found on the side of the freeway was Mary Weathers. He then told him that the DNA that was found in her mouth and under her nails did not belong to her. He also informed him that they had put samples of the DNA in the criminal database but found no match.

The last thing he told Peterson was that there were two sets of finger prints found on her car. He informed him that one set belonged to her and the other set belonged to a person unknown. Peterson thanked him for his help then hung the phone up.

He pulled out a pen and pad and started jotting things that the expert had told him down. Perkins asked him, "So what did you get?" He held his finger up indicating for her to hold on, then picked the phone up and dialed another number.

That time he called Samantha Stevens and she informed him that she could not do anything with the video from the parking lot. She told him that the resolution on the film was too low and she explained to him that she faired better with the footage from inside of the store. She told him that although the film was still fuzzy, you could make out the images a little better. She let him know that she was sending the footage back to him as an email attachment.

Peterson told her, "Samantha thanks," He was surprised when she responded with no attitude in her voice telling him, "You're welcome."

He used his finger to push down the button on the phone, when the line was clear he called back down to forensics and asked the receptionist the extension for Norman.

Norman answered the phone and Peterson asked him, "What do you got for me?"

"Just the DNA results from the body pieces that we found at the dump. The dental records prove that they belong to Helen Morgan."

"Okay, thanks Norman."

"Pete, before you go, have you guys found the rest of the body yet?"

"No, we haven't found it yet Norm." Peterson told him then hung up.

He turned to Perkins and said, "So this is what we got, we have a positive ID on Morgan and Weathers. The DNA found in Weathers mouth did not register in the criminal's database. Also, there were two sets of prints on her car, one belonged to her and the other to a person unknown. Last Stevenson, says she couldn't do anything with the video from the parking lot, but she said that she was able to enhance the video from inside the store a little bit. She is going to send it back to me attached to an email."

Peterson reclined back in his chair, put both of his hands behind his head and clasped them together. He closed his eyes for a minute, to clear his head. Perkins asked him, "Pete what's wrong?"

"I'm just thinking about how we got so much work to do. We got so many things to do that I don't even know where to start."

"What are the things that have to be done?"

"We have to deliver the bad news to Weathers' family, we need to go back up to the hospital, and we have to view the footage from the store. It's just so many things."

"How about we split up for today? We can cover more ground that way. You go back up to the hospital and I will go inform the family about Weathers. We can meet back here after that, and then take it from there."

Peterson considered her plan, which sounded good accept for the part about letting her go inform the family.

He knew that Perkins could be a little insensitive when it carries to dealing with men. He did not consider Cody Miller to be a suspect at that time and he was afraid that if he let Perkins deliver the news, she might treat him as if he was one.

He also knew that if he denied her request, it would bring friction between them. Peterson was almost certain that she would become upset and feel as if he did not think she was competent enough to do her job.

It had taken over a year for her to warm up to him and he did not want their relationship to take any steps backwards.

He decided that it would be best to accept her offer. He told her, "That sounds like a plan."

Perkins knew that Peterson really did not want to let her to go inform the family, but she was happy that he had trusted her to handle something alone.

Perkins did not like the fact that she was always in his shadow. She understood that he had seniority and was the lead detective, but she felt like a secretary working with him. She was tired of only taking information down and playing the sidekick.

She yearned to get from under his shadow and be able to get out into the field by herself. She was just happy that she was finally getting a chance to prove herself.

Since they shared an unmarked car, Perkins decided to drive her own car. She got in it and headed up to Cody Miller's residence.

22

While Peterson and Perkins were out following up on leads, the Cleveland police department and several other law enforcement persons were at a factory that manufactured vacuum cleaners.

They were called after a homeless man informed a manager at the plant that he found a part of a dead body inside of the dumpster that sat on their property.

After being notified by the homeless man, the manager did not even think of taking a look for himself. Instead, he told the homeless man not to go anywhere and he went back inside and called authorities.

Within half an hour the factory's parking lot was filled with all kind of law enforcement officers. CSI investigators climbed into the dumpster and pulled the garbage bag that contained the midsection of a body out. They placed the bag onto the ground, and then climbed back into the dumpster looking for the rest of the body. They tore open every bag that was inside of the dumpster, but did not find any other body parts.

Two detectives questioned the homeless man. The detective's names were Sanchez and Murphy. Sanchez did most of the questioning. He asked the man his name and he responded that his name was Ralph.

He began to question him, "Okay, Ralph could you tell us what your purpose was when you climbed into the dumpster?"

"I'm homeless and I search most of the factories in this industrial area, looking for anything that is edible. I also look for anything that has any value to it, such as aluminum cans."

A worker from the factory vouched for Ralph telling the detectives that he frequently climbed into the dumpsters on the property. He told the officers that there had been many times when management had chased Ralph off the property.

The detectives thanked the employee for his help, and they took all of Ralph's personal information down. They also wanted to know where he laid his head at night. When the detectives were through with Ralph and the body parts had been taken from the scene the detectives went back to headquarters.

When they got there Sanchez sent out a bulletin to all the precincts in Cleveland as well as notifying other police departments in the surrounding areas of their find.

The captain at Peterson's and Perkins' precinct got the bulletin and he sent a response back. In the response he let the detectives know that two detectives from his precinct were investigating a murder case in which only the limbs and head had been found. He informed the detective of the fact that the body parts were at the morgue and DNA samples were at the forensics lab. He also informed him that he would have his detectives contact him as soon as they got back to the precinct.

Sanchez was glad that the captain from the second precinct notified him about the case that two of his detectives were investigating. The captain told him that his detectives were investigating a case where they had every body part, except for the torso. Sanchez appreciated the captain's help but he had no intentions of waiting for the captain's detectives to call him. Sanchez was an ambitious person and he knew that he was going to be up for a promotion in the upcoming months.

He seen the case that he had just been given, as being a big one. He thought that the killings could be the work of a serial killer in the making. He knew that if he could blow the case wide open before the killer got a chance to strike again, that he would surely get the promotion that he so badly wanted.

Soon as he had gotten off the phone with the captain, he called down to the morgue and over to forensics. He wanted the people at the morgue to see if the body parts that they had on ice, matched the torso that they had just received. He wanted forensics to compare the DNA from the body parts, with the DNA from the torso.

When he had everything in the works, he turned to his partner Murphy and said, "The ball is rolling, let's go and crack this case." Together they left downtown headquarters and headed to the city's morgue.

23

Peterson arrived at Metropolitan hospital and caught the elevator up to the sixth floor. He intended to re-interview some of Mary Weathers' co-workers. He wanted to see if any of them had remembered anything that they might have failed to remember the first time they were interviewed.

Peterson explained to all the staff that Weathers' had been brutally murdered. Most of the staff could not believe that she had actually been killed. A lot of the woman staff became scared when they found out she had been kidnapped from the hospital's parking garage. That made them feel unsafe.

Even after disclosing to the staff that Weathers had been murdered and thrown onto the side of the freeway, Peterson still did not get any useful information. He decided to try questioning workers on some of the other floors to see if he could gather any leads.

Since Weathers had disappeared from the third level parking garage, he decided to question some of the staff on that floor next.

He caught the elevator down to the third floor and went to the nurse's station.

He pulled Weathers' picture out and started showing it to some of the staff asking them if they remember her.

He was showing a group of staff members her picture, when Dr. Rebecca Rogers came walking down the corridor.

Dr. Rogers seen the people gathered in the group as she was walking down the hallway. She decided to approach them to see what was going on.

When she got there she asked them what was going on and detective Peterson showed her the picture and asked her if she remembered the woman in it. Dr. Rogers took the picture and looked at it and instantly recognized Mary Weathers.

She had heard about Weathers' disappearance and had been wondering if they had located her. Dr. Rogers and Weathers had never been friends, but they had always been cordial with each other. She asked the detective, "You guys have not found her yet?"

"Yes, we have found her. We found her brutally murdered and discarded on the side of the 480 freeway."

Rebecca felt her body start to shake. In her job she dealt with death every day, but for her to hear that someone that she had actually known was brutally murdered rattled her. She felt that it was a shame that a person could not even be totally safe at their place of work.

She wished that she could do something that would be helpful to the detective. They were all standing there talking, when she spotted Dr. James Mitchel coming down the hallway.

James noticed her at the same time that she saw him. His reaction when he saw her was to turn and head in the other direction. Just when he was about to turn around she called out to him, "Hey Dr. Mitchel, could I see you over here for a minute." James knew that he was busted, so he walked over to the group of people.

When he got there, Dr. Rogers introduced him to detective Peterson, "Dr. Mitchel this is detective Peterson and he is investigating the disappearance and the murder of Mary Weathers. Someone brutally killed her James. You remember her don't you?" James tried to act like he was trying to recall the name and after a few seconds he said, "I can't remember anyone by that name."

"Sure you remember her James." Dr. Rogers said to him, then turned to the detective and said, "Could you show him the picture?" Peterson said, "Sure" then held the picture out for him to take it. James put his hand out and accepted the picture. He looked at it and pretended like he was really studying it. After he pretended for what seemed like eternity, he gave the photo back to the detective and said, "I still don't remember her."

Dr. Rogers decided to help him with his memory, "You have to remember her, and she was one of the nurses that assisted you in performing that triple bypass surgery that you performed last year. You had spoken highly of her afterwards and you were disappointed when you found out that she had been transferred to the sixth floor."

James knew that he was behaving suspiciously. He realized that Rebecca wasn't going to let it go until he admitted that he knew the woman. He asked the detective if he could look at the picture again and he handed it back to him.

James looked at the picture again and that time he let his face show a sign of recognition. He snapped his fingers on his right hand twice then said, "Okay yes, I remember her now. It's been a while, at least a year since I have seen her. You say she was killed?"

"She was kidnapped from the third level parking garage, then she was killed and thrown onto the side of the freeway."

"You can't be serious, can you?"

"I'm very serious Dr. Mitchel!"

"Well, how can I be of help detective?" he asked Peterson.

"We are trying to find anybody who may have noticed anyone acting strange, hanging around the third level of the parking garage last Thursday."

"I wish I could be of help to you detective, but I park on the first level of the parking garage. Peterson thought to himself that it was time to move onto another floor. He had talked to most of the staff on the third floor and had come up with nothing. He told everyone thanks for their help, and then he walked to the elevator.

The group of staff members started dispersing and James took off walking fast down the corridor. He did not know it right away but Rebecca was right on his heels. He was walking so fast that she had to call out to him, "James, where are you in a rush to?" Without stopping or looking back, James responded by saying, "I'm late for an appointment. I will talk to you later." Rebecca stopped in her tracks and watched him as he walked quickly down the hall, then turned the corner.

Even though he was then out of her sight, Rebecca stood there for a few more minutes, it was something about the way James had been acting lately that was bothering her. She knew that something was going on with him and she intended to find out what it was. She turned then headed for her office.

λ

Perkins arrived at Cody Miller's residence. She got out of her car and walked up to his door as if she had a purpose. She knocked on the door and after a few seconds she heard footsteps approaching it. The footsteps stopped when they got to the door then someone asked, "Who is it?"

"It is detective Perkins." she responded. Perkins heard a chain being removed from the door, then the sound of a lock turning. Cody Miller opened the door wearing nothing but a pair of boxer shorts and a t-shirt.

The way he was dressed did not matter to Perkins, but the way he looked did. To Perkins it looked as if his conscience was eating at him. She took in the following facts, he had not shaved in a couple days, his hair was unkept and he had bags under both of his eyes. To her those were the signs of his guilty conscience eating at him.

Cody did not like her, but he politely asked her, "How can I help you detective?"

"Are your fiancé's parents here?"

"No they are not."

"What about her sister?" Cody looked at her strangely then replied, "No she isn't here either. They are all over at Rachel's house."

"That's good because I would like to talk to you alone. Is it possible for me to come in and talk to you?"

"Have you guys found Mary?"

"No we haven't, but I would like to talk to you about her for a minute if you don't mind?" Cody opened the door wide and allowed her to enter. After she entered, he closed the door, went over to the couch and flopped down on it. He did not even offer Perkins a seat, so she remained standing.

Perkins stood in the middle of the living room just looking around. She was looking for anything that she could find that would link Cody to his fiancé's murder.

Cody noticed how she was just standing there looking around his residence. He said to her, "Detective you said that you wanted to talk to me. You did not mention anything about sightseeing."

"Well, Mr. Miller I have some bad news for you."

"Get to the point detective."

"We found your fiancé." Hearing those words, Cody became anxious to know where Mary was. He jumped up off the couch and asked Perkins, "So where is she?"

"She is down at the city morgue."

"What!" Cody stated then put his hands up over his face. He started pacing back and forth in his living room saying to himself, "No, it can't be! It just can't be! We were supposed to be married in two months."

Perkins just stood there watching him. She was trying to determine if he was being truly sincere or faking. Cody stopped pacing, then turned to Perkins and asked her, "Should I call her family?"

"I think it would be best if you allow me to tell them. I wanted to ask you if you are willing to consent to taking a DNA test and to be fingerprinted."

"What! Why are you asking me that? Am I a suspect or something?"

"We just want to eliminate you from being a suspect?"

"Detective this is crazy. You have come to my home and told me that my fiancé has evidently been murdered, then you turnaround and tell me that I'm a suspect."

"Mr. Miller all you have to do is consent to the test and you can easily be in the clear." Tears started to fall from Cody's eyes and he started pacing the floor again. As he paced he rubbed both of his hands through his unkept hair. He stopped abruptly and turned towards

Perkins, "Okay detective, when can we get this done, so that I will be able to mourn my fiancé properly?"

"If you get dressed, I will take you down to the station or you can follow me in your car."

"I will follow you. Just let me get dressed, and then we can clear up this ridiculous accusation." Cody went upstairs, brushed his teeth, washed his face then got dressed. After he was dressed he grabbed his keys and together he and Perkins left his house heading down to the station.

Cody was highly upset about the accusations, but he was willing to do anything to clear his name. He just hoped that the ludicrous accusation did not get back to his fiancé's parents.

They got down to the station and he signed some consent papers. After he signed the papers, Perkins had him fingerprinted and swabbed. Once they were done both Cody and Perkins left the station. Cody headed back home and Perkins headed to the home of Rachel Weathers to inform Mary Weathers' family about her death.

24

James and Jerry were at home arguing. They were down in Jerry's office arguing about everything that had taken place over the past week. James started becoming frantic after he had watched the news report about the body parts being found at the city dump. He was trying to get Jerry to see what his demonic behavior was causing.

Jerry listened to James talk about his encounter with the police. He told Jerry how he had tried to deny knowing the murdered woman, but that Dr. Rogers had put him on blast.

Jerry started thinking, that if anybody was to be their downfall, that it would be James. They sat there arguing back and forth.

"Can't you see what your madness is doing? There are police roaming all over the hospital asking questions. I was put under the gun by one of the staff. Did I forget to mention that the police found pieces of a body at the city dump? I knew this would happen!" James said to Jerry.

"James, nothing I have done will bring us down. It is your weakness that is going to bring us down. You have always been weak when it came to women and you still are. That Rebecca woman has your card. She is a nosy, snooping bitch and if you would have let me handle her in the beginning, then there wouldn't have been a need for me to snatch the Weathers woman."

"When are you going to start accepting responsibility? It's nobody's fault but yours. You are the one that's sick, not me. They are still looking for that woman's torso. What did you do with it?"

"I fed it to the fishes in Lake Erie."

"You are really demonic!"

"And you're just a weak little boy."

"Just because I care what happens to people doesn't make me weak."

"James you are very weak and your weakness shows through everything you do. It shows in your voice, through your body language and your behavior. Dr. Rogers can tell that something is going on with you. She can tell that you have been acting different lately. I can tell you this she is not going to stop until she finds out what's going on with you. I think it's time you let me take care of her before she brings us both down."

James felt his body start to shake and he began to hyperventilate. Both of them were things he did when he became nervous.

He felt that there was no way that he could let Jerry do Rebecca any harm. He acknowledged the fact that she did stick her nose in places that she shouldn't, but he did not feel that she deserved to die because of it.

He told Jerry, "I'm not going to let you do any harm to Rebecca you have done enough harm already."

"Suit yourself James, but if she leads to our downfall, it's going to be on your shoulders, not mine. From this point on don't you bitch at me about anything. I have yet to bring any heat on us and if you are going to let a snooping bitch become our downfall then that's on you. Now if you will excuse me, I have work to do."

James was tired of arguing, so he turned around and headed back upstairs. He went up to his bedroom, popped two valiums then he went to lie down on his bed. He laid there thinking about what Jerry had said and he started to wonder if Rebecca would indeed become their downfall. He fell asleep before he could reach a conclusion.

λ

Peterson arrived back at the station and went straight to his desk. He wanted to see if he had received the video footage back from Samantha.

He sat down, booted up his computer and found that be had several emails. Before he got a chance to open any of them the desk sergeant popped up at his desk and said, "Peterson the captain wants to see you ASAP!"

"What does he want to see me about?"

"I don't know, but whatever it is it seems to be urgent."

Peterson got up from his computer and took off heading for the captain's office. On his way there be tried to remember if he had recently done anything wrong. He knew that most times when the captain requested to see you that you were in hot water. He could not think of anything that he had done wrong. His thoughts went to Perkins and he started hoping that she did not cause any trouble when she went to inform the Weathers' family of her death.

When he got to the captain's office, he informed his secretary that he had been summoned by the captain. The secretary picked up the phone and notified the captain that he was there. She hung the phone up and before she could say anything to Peterson, the captain's door opened and he stepped out and told Peterson to come in.

Peterson entered the office and the captain closed the door. He walked over to his desk and sat down. Peterson walked over to the front of his desk and was about to take a seat when the captain told him, "That won't be necessary. You won't be here long." Peterson remained standing and the captain asked him, "Have you made any headway in the case where only the limbs and head were found?"

"I was in the mist of following up on some leads when I was summoned to your office sir."

"Well a detective name Sanchez from down at headquarters sent out a bulletin saying that they had just removed a torso from a garbage bin that sits on a factory that produces vacuum cleaners parking lot. I talked to the detective myself and told him that you were investigating a case in which only the limbs and head were found. I also informed him that I would have you contact him soon as you got in. Here, this is his number." The captain told him as be held out a paper with a number on it.

Peterson took the paper from the captain, and then he continued, "I'm advising you to contact him immediately, so that you can get this case closed. Its bringing too much unwanted attention to the department and unwanted attention is not good for us caprenda?"

"I'll get right on it cap!" Peterson told him.

The captain got up from his desk, walked over to the door and opened it. Peterson stepped out his office and started to walk away, when the captain called his name, "Peterson!" he stopped, turned around and said, "Yes Cap?"

"I'm counting on you."

"I won't let you down sir." He replied then stepped out into the hall. He decided that he was going to check his emails later. He decided to head straight to the city morgue.

Peterson was walking past the sergeant's desk, when he called out to him, "Peterson let Perkins know that those fingerprints did match the car." Peterson was baffled by what the staff sergeant had just said. He stopped in his tracks, turned to the sergeant and asked, "What prints?"

"The fingerprints she had taken from Cody Miller, matched the other set that was found on Weathers' car."

"When was Cody Miller down here?"

"She brought him in earlier. They came in together and left together." Peterson was starting to regret letting Perkins go by herself to inform Weathers' family and her fiancé of her death. Perkins had done just what he had expected her to do, which was to treat Miller like a suspect. He knew he did not have time to worry about it right then, he had more important things to take care of. He told the desk sergeant, "If I see her before you do I will tell her and if you see her before I do, please tell her I said to meet me at the county morgue," then he headed out to his car.

Once inside of his car and heading to the morgue, he pulled his phone off his hip and called the number the captain had given him. He dialed the number twice and got Sanchez's answering machine each time. He figured that he was already at the morgue.

When he got to the morgue he approached the security station that sat right inside of the entrance. He showed the guard his credentials, and then told him why he was there. The guard told him, "Two other detectives and a guy from forensics are down there with the medical examiner. They are in room 2B, which is right down the hall on your left."

"Thank you," Peterson told him then headed down the hall. He found room 2B and pushed open the swinging doors to enter. When he entered there were four people inside of the room. There were the two detectives, the medical examiner and a forensics expert.

Peterson had seen two rolling slabs that were almost next to each other. The only thing that separated them was the medical examiner that stood in between them. On one table were the limbs and the head from the case Peterson was investigating. On the other table was the torso that had been recovered earlier that day.

When Peterson entered everyone except for the examiner, who was trying to piece the body together, turned to face him. Peterson walked over and introduced himself.

"I'm detective Peterson from the second precinct." Two of the three returned his introduction. Peterson noticed that the overweight Spanish guy was looking at him as if he had a problem with him being there. He being the only person in the room of Spanish descent, Peterson pegged him to be Sanchez.

He turned towards him and said, "You are Sanchez I presume?"

"Yeah, I'm Sanchez, what of it?" Peterson found that he did not like Sanchez's attitude. He figured that if the man didn't tighten his attitude up, then he would have to give him a little attitude adjustment.

Peterson continued, "Apparently you talked to my captain earlier."

"Okay?"

"Well then you know that I am the lead detective on the case that involves the limbs and the head that are on that slab?" Sanchez did not like the words that Peterson was using.

The words lead detective held no weight with him. He had no intentions on sharing the case or credit for solving it with anybody other than his partner.

He told Peterson, "We were assigned to this case by our superiors down at headquarters."

"You may have been assigned to investigating the case involving the torso, but there is no way you were assigned to take over my case. If worst come to worst we might end up working together but you are not taking the case from me. Besides, I already have some evidence that may prove the identity of the killer."

All while they were arguing, the examiner had been trying to piece the body parts together. He had become disturbed when he found that the limbs and head did not come from that torso. No part of the limbs or the head connected with the torso. He also found that neither color of the skin nor the texture of it matched.

While he was working he was listening to the two detectives going at it and figured that it was time to stop them from arguing for nothing. He turned to them and said, "Excuse me gentlemen, but the two of you seem to be arguing for no reason." Both Sanchez and Peterson stopped talking and turned towards the examiner. Sanchez asked him, "What are you talking about doc?"

The examiner pointed to the body parts that were on the table then said, "Those limbs, nor the head came from that torso." Everybody in the room was stung by the examiner's words.

"Are you sure doc?" Sanchez asked him, while seeing a vision in his head of his promotion going down the drain.

"I'm 100% positive that these body parts are not from this torso. If you will come closer I will show you how the bones from the torso and the limbs were severed differently." Everybody that were in the room closed in around the table that had the limbs and the torso on it. The medical examiner proceeded to prove his point. He picked up an arm and showed the area where the limb had been severed to them.

"Gentlemen if you will look closely, you will see that this limb was severed evenly and cleanly. Whoever severed this limb was an expert in the human anatomy. Each of these limbs was cut cleanly. The perp as you would call him severed all of these limbs by cutting through the joints, ligaments, and the tendons that connected the bones to the body. No parts of the bones were cut."

After they all had a chance to see what he was explaining to them, he set the arm back onto the table. Then he used both of his hands to lift the upper part of the torso up off the table. He explained to them what he wanted them to take notice of.

"Now for this torso, whoever removed the limbs from it used a totally different method. They did not use precision and also they used torturous measures in removing the limbs. If you will look at the socket of the shoulder, you will see that the flesh has been seared. I had to cut through the burned flesh to get to the bone. The left socket for the leg was the only severed area that had not been burned."

"Excuse me doc, but could you explain why someone would burn those areas?" Peterson asked him.

"My guess is, whoever removed the limbs burned the areas afterwards to keep the victim from bleeding out."

"So you're saying the victim was alive when she had her limbs removed?"

"That is my conclusion, whoever killed the person that this torso belongs to, wanted that person to suffer."

They wanted to keep the victim alive as long as they could so they could continue to inflict pain on them. Now if you will let me finish, I will point out some other facts for you."

"Please continue doc," Sanchez said while casting an evil look Peterson's way.

The medical examiner continued, "Also whoever removed the limbs from the torso cut straight through the bones. They also cut through the bones at slanted angles. Again if you would look closely, you will see that the clavicle bone, which is the shoulder bone, was cut at a forty-five degree angle."

After letting them see what he was talking about, he sat the top half of the torso down. He went to the bottom half, lifted it, and then told them, "If you would look closely, you will see that the pelvic bone was cut the same way. There is another difference between the limbs and the torso. If you look closely, you will see that the color of the skin is a different shade and the textures of the skin are different." The detectives and the forensics expert all observed and understood every point that the medical examiner made.

Peterson still wanted to be clear, so he asked, "Doc so what is your overall conclusion?"

"My overall conclusion is you need to be out there looking for another set of limbs and another torso."

"One last question doc. Could this still be the work of one killer, or should we be looking for two different killers?"

"There are a couple common links between the cases. Even though the person who severed the limbs used precision in removing them, he still exhibited a sadistic nature by removing the eyes out of the skull. It should be noted, that the killer used an object that was as sharp as a scalpel to remove them. Also the same kind of tool seems to have been used in both cases. My guess is it was a power saw. With the common links versus the different methods used, it's hard to tell. If it is one killer involved in both crimes, I would think that he has a psychotic disorder. My guess is that he is either a schizophrenic or is bipolar. If these killings are the work of two different killers, then I think that you gentlemen have your hands full."

Peterson looked at Sanchez and said, "Looks like we are going to be investigating cases that may share a common link."

Sanchez sneered at Peterson's remark, but knew that Peterson was probably right. Since Peterson told him that he had evidence that may help them identify the killer he figured that it would be best to join forces with him. He thought about the saying, "If you can't beat them, you might as well join them."

He turned to Peterson then said to him, "We should have a press conference to let the public know what's going on. We may be able to flush him or them out." Peterson thought about what the captain had told him regarding unwanted attention then he responded saying, "Your actions could backfire. You could start a public panic and send the killer or killers underground."

"The public has the right to know what's going on."

"Be my guess then, I just won't have any part of it." Peterson decided to go talk to the forensics expert, who was taking DNA samples from the torso. He wanted to find out when the results would be in. The expert told him it was going to take at least 72-hours. After hearing that Peterson left out of the morgue.

Sanchez used the morgue's phone to call every news station in Cleveland, Ohio. He told each of them that he was holding a press conference about a possible serial killer being on the loose. He told them that he would be holding the conference in one hour on the steps of the county morgue.

Sanchez wasn't really concerned about the public safety. He viewed violent crimes and murders as being means of job security. He really wanted the attention that was going to come with making the case public. He wanted to showboat and have his face all over the news.

Peterson was sitting in his car, battling with his conscience. Something kept telling him not to leave. He really wanted to hear what Sanchez had to say to the reporters. He decided to sit in his car and wait for the news media to arrive, so that he could watch the jerk Sanchez, hold the conference.

Within forty-five minutes the front of the morgue was packed with cameramen and news reporters. Spectators that were walking by seen all of the cameras and decided to stop and see what was going on.

After all the news crews had assembled in front of the morgue, Sanchez stepped out of the morgue's door.

Peterson sat in his car and watched Sanchez walk out onto the steps of the morgue as if he was a superstar stepping out to the world premiere of his movie. Peterson just shook his head, because he could clearly see that Sanchez loved the limelight. He decided to get out of the car and go stand in the crowd to listen to what he had to say.

Sanchez walked down to the bottom step, so that he could be close to the reporter's mics. He started the conference with, "I have called you people from the news media, so that through you, we can inform the public of some horrific events that have taken place in our city. There have been two murders in which the bodies were totally dismembered. We have yet to recover some of the body parts."

A reporter from the eight o'clock news quickly jumped in and asked a question, "Detective you say you're still looking for some body parts?"

"Yes we are,"

"Do you think because both bodies were dismembered, that these killings are connected? And if so do you think we have a serial killer on our hands?"

"As of right now, we are not 100% sure if we are dealing with one or two killers and nothing suggest that we are dealing with a serial killer."

Peterson's attention was on Sanchez, when he felt a tap on his shoulder, he turned around and found Perkins standing there. She asked him, "What's going on?"

"I'll explain it to you after that fool up there gets through talking." Perkins positioned herself next to him and together they watched Sanchez perform.

A reporter for channel five news asked Sanchez, "Do authorities have any leads in the case?" Sanchez remembered what Peterson told him about having evidence that could lead to the killer and he decided to act as if it was him that had the evidence. He told the reporter, "We have evidence that we are looking at right now that could lead to the killer or killers. It's only a matter of time before we track the person or persons down."

Sanchez felt like a celebrity in front of the cameras. He loved the attention that he was getting. He answered a few more of the reporters' questions, and then he closed the conference out by looking into the camera and saying, "Whoever you are, you're a sick individual and we are not going to stop until we catch you." After that Sanchez parted the reporters and pushed his way through the crowd with his partner at his side.

Peterson turned and walked back over to his car with Perkins following him. When they got to his car, Perkins asked him, "What was that all about?"

"It was about a detective that really wanted to be a celebrity."

"What was all that talk about there being two dis-membered bodies?"

"A torso was removed from a dumpster that sits on a vacuum cleaner's factory parking lot. That's why I'm down here, we were sure that it was the missing torso that the limbs and head had been removed from."

"And you are saying that they did not come from it?"

"That's what I'm saying. We were shocked by the medical examiner's findings, but they were accurate."

"So there are still some limbs and another torso out there?"

"That is correct." Perkins mind started turning fast. What she had just found out made her question her theory of Miller being the killer of his fiancé. Peterson knew what she was thinking and he told her, "Before I forget, the serge said to tell you that Miller's prints matched the other set that was found on Weathers' car." Perkins looked up at Peterson and tried to read his face. She did not like the look that he had on it, so she asked him, "You think I was wrong to   ask him to be printed and to take a DNA test?"

Peterson frowned then wanted to make sure that he had heard her right, "You had him take a DNA test?"

"He consented to it, besides you said that his prints came back on her car."

"Perkins, he is her fiancé, his prints being on her car is no big deal. Plus he said he stopped and checked her car out, the day that he came down to the station. If you're wrong on this and he gets himself a lawyer the department is going to get a lot of flak behind it."

"Well, I done made my bed so I guess I have to lie in it."

"We need to be getting back to the precinct. I want to look at the video feed, from inside of the store."

Peterson got into his car and Perkins got into hers, then they both headed to their precinct.

λ

While driving, Perkins thought about everything that she had just learned. She hoped that the DNA that was found under Weathers' fingernails and in her mouth belonged to Miller. She knew that if it didn't come back to him that meant she had jumped the gun and her actions were going to bring flack to the department. She started wondering if she was letting the personal events that she had experienced in her life cause her to be bias in doing her job.

She knew that she would soon have to figure that question out. If it did become apparent to her that she was letting her personal experiences interfere with her job, then she knew that it would be time for her to look for another job. She silently said a prayer as she followed Peterson to the precinct.

25

There were two people who watched the live press conference and became upset by it. One of those people was the city mayor. Soon as the conference came on he received a phone call telling him to turn the television inside of his office on and to turn it to the news.

He picked the remote up off of his desk, then turned the television on and found that he did not have to flick through channels to find out what was going on. When he looked at the screen he could clearly see that every news station in Cleveland was there.

He sat on the edge of his desk and watched as a fat, Spanish detective talked about a possible serial killer or killers being on the loose. The mayor was about to be up for re-election in the upcoming months. He felt that he did not need the city thinking that the citizens weren't safe. His first campaign had been based on guaranteeing public safety.

He was upset at the idiot that was on TV putting the city of Cleveland in an uproar. He used the remote to shut the TV off, and then he snatched up the phone and placed a call down to police headquarters. He dialed the direct line to the captain's office and he answered, "Captain Lewis."

The mayor got straight to the point. He asked the captain, "Harry tell me that you did not approve the press conference that some asshole detective just had on the steps of the county morgue?"

The captain was baffled by what the mayor was telling him. He knew nothing about a press conference being held. He knew one thing though, if the mayor chewed him out, then whoever was behind the press conference were getting a hole chewed in their ass. He told the mayor, "Sir I did not give approval for any press conference to be given. You are the first person that has even brought it to my attention."

"Harry, I'm up for re-election in a few months. I don't need a fame seeking detective putting this city in an uproar and putting my career in jeopardy."

"Mayor, I apologize for whoever the jerk is. I promise you that I will find out who is behind it, and some heads will roll."

"Right now, I want you to do damage control and I want an arrest made as soon as possible, so that this thing quickly blows over. Do whatever you need to do to make an arrest, do I make myself clear?"

"I understand everything that you are saying sir and I will get right on it."

"You better!" the mayor said then slammed the phone down.

The captain made a call to homicide and found out who the detectives were that was assigned to the murder case. He found out that it was Sanchez and Murphy. He ordered that as soon as they entered the building, they were to be notified to report straight to his office.

The other person that was upset by the conference was Jerry. He had sat in the living room watching the live news conference and he was happy to see that his killings were making headlines. Seeing the detective talking about his work made him happy, but his happiness quickly changed to anger. His mood swiftly changed when the detective looked into the camera and referred to him as being sick and demented.

He hated for people to call him or refer to him as being sick or crazy. Watching the fat man on TV talk to the reporters, Jerry concluded that there was no way the fat, incompetent detective could catch him.

He decided that he was going to give the detective another reason to refer to him as being sick. He felt that he had been quiet long enough and he decided that it was time to speak again.

He already had a patient in mind, when he crept upstairs to James' room. He quietly entered his room, went over and lifted his keys off the nightstand. He walked back over to the door, then turned and looked at James. He stood and watched him lying on the bed sleeping peacefully, and then he smiled and left the room. He left the house, heading to snatch up his next unsuspecting victim.

As soon as Peterson and Perkins arrived at the precinct, the desk sergeant informed them that the captain wanted to see them in his office immediately.

He did not even allow them to stop at their desk he escorted them straight to the captain's office. While they were walking to the captain's office, both Peterson and Perkins were trapped in their own thoughts. Perkins was wondering if they were about to be chewed out because of her treating Miller as a suspect.

Peterson figured he knew why they were being summoned. He was one hundred percent sure that it revolved around what had taken place at the morgue.

They were almost to the captain's office, when his secretary looked up and seen them approaching. She did not even wait for them to reach her desk, before she picked up the phone and notified the captain.

By the time they reached the secretary's desk, the captain's door was open and he was standing in it.

He stood in his doorway, with an angry look on his face. Both detectives could tell by his facial expression, that trouble was brewing.

When they reached his door, the captain looked in both of their faces then said to them, "Both of you knuckleheads get in here." The sergeant felt that his job was done, so he turned and headed back to his desk."

The captain stepped aside, so that they could enter. He noticed as they walked by him, that they had gloomy expressions on their faces. After they entered, he closed the door and told them, "You two might as well take those sad looks off of your faces." He walked around his desk, sat down in his chair and put both of his hands on his desk. He then looked at Peterson and asked him, "Peterson did we or did we not just have a conversation earlier today about having unwanted attention on us?"

"I had nothing to do with that sir. I tried to talk that idiot out of it, but he was set on becoming a celebrity."

"That's funny, because he told his captain that it was all your idea, for him to hold the press conference."

"What! That fat weasel! I swear to you cap, I had no part in what he did."

"It doesn't matter one way or the other. It wasn't too long ago, that I hung up from having a conference call with the mayor and the captain down at headquarters. The mayor wants this case closed fast."

"We are diligently working the case." Peterson told him.

"You're not working fast enough. He wants this case closed out within seventy two hours."

"That's not possible. It's going to take that long to get the DNA results back."

"Don't worry about that, orders went over to the CSI unit, straight from the mayor's office, telling them to expedite the testing. By lunch time tomorrow, the results will be on your desk. Until then, you two need to be looking for other evidence that will help you solve those cases." He stopped talking, and looked from Peterson to Perkins, and then he asked them, "Do I make myself clear?" Simultaneously they both answered, "Yes."

"You two are dismissed, get back to work." They left his office, heading back to their desk. Perkins was relieved that what they got chewed out about, she wasn't involved in. She was glad that there was no mention of Cody Miller.

Peterson on the other hand was extremely hot under the collar. He could not believe that the fat, slime ball Sanchez, had pinned everything on him. He had thoughts of ringing the fat detective's neck the next time he saw him.

When Peterson got to his desk he turned his computer on and started opening up his emails. The second email he opened came from Samantha Stevens. When he opened it he found that there were two pictures attached to it. Stevens had enhanced the images on the video and printed them out. He looked at them and seen that they were still fuzzy. Although you could somewhat see the people in the pictures, they still weren't clear enough to make a positive identification. Peterson knew that it was going to take somebody that actually knew the people in the pictures to identify them.

He saw that there was a note attached to one of the pictures and he read it. The note was from Stevens, telling him that those were the best shots on the video.

Peterson seen that one picture gave a side view of the man standing by himself and the other showed him accompanying Weathers out of the store. Peterson found himself staring at the picture that showed the front of the man's face. Even with the picture not being clear, for some reason the person in the picture seemed familiar to him.

He kept looking at the picture trying to find a clue that would tell him why the man in the picture looked so familiar. After he studied the picture for what had seemed like forever, he decided that he would release the images to the media and see if someone that knew the man would identify him.

He called all of the news stations and told them that he was faxing over two pictures of the man that was the suspect in the killing of a woman whose body was dismembered. He informed the news stations that when they showed the pictures, to ask that any viewer who could identify the man in the picture to call his number at homicide.

He gave the news stations his number at the department, and then he hung up and faxed them the pictures.

He was sitting at his desk, when once again he found himself picking the photos up and studying them. He was studying them in hopes that something would jar his memory.

Perkins had seen how he kept studying the two pictures and asked him, "Are you onto something?"

"For some reason the man in these pictures seem familiar to me." Perkins went back over to her computer and finished filling out her daily reports.

Peterson kept studying the pictures for almost two hours.

Perkins had finished her reports and shut her computer off. It was only five minutes left before their shift ended. She walked over to Peterson and said, "It's quitting time. You might as well give your eyes a rest. Go home and get some sleep and whatever it is that you are trying to remember might come back to you."

Peterson figured she was right, so he shut his computer off and prepared to leave also. He thought if he gave his brain some rest, that he might be able to figure out why the man in the picture seemed so familiar. Together him and Perkins left the precinct and headed home.

26

It was almost midnight and Jerry was parked across the street from the one story home. The home belonged to the person that he intended to make his next patient.

A couple hours earlier, he had sat outside of the woman's house job. He waited for her to get off work, so that he could follow her home and apprehend her.

He knew that if he did not take care of her, James weakness for her would bring them both down. To him, James mind was twisted. He could not understand how James actually believed that he was protecting them both.

Jerry thought James had to be losing his mind to be thinking that way. He felt that it was him who was protecting them. He said to himself, "I have been protecting us both for years. I have been saving him from his weaknesses. It was my job back then and it's still my job now."

He sat there until the woman got off work, then followed her home. When they arrived at her home, he waited ten minutes after she entered her home, before he exited the car and headed over to her house. Before he left the car he put on his Isotoner gloves, grabbed the pieces of rope and a pouch that held four slim metal strips off the passenger's seat. When he got to the side of her house, he monitored her movement by watching the lights that she turned on.

He went to the window of the room that he seen the last light come on. He crouched outside of that window for a few minutes, and then he rose up just enough so that his eyes could see over the window seal.

The curtains on the window were slightly parted and he found that she was inside of her bedroom. He stayed crouched low and watched the woman as she undressed.

The woman stripped completely naked, then walked out of her bedroom. Jerry figured that she was heading to the bathroom to take either a bath or a shower.

He looked to see what light would come on next so that he would know her location. When the light came on, still crouched low he went to the window where the light was coming from. He found that it was a small window with a frosted pane, which prevented him from being able to see inside of it. Although he could not see through the window, he could hear the sounds of the running water. He listened to the sound of the water running and wondered exactly what she was doing. After about fifteen minutes the water shut off, then after two more minutes the lights in the room went out.

Jerry figured that it could only be one place that she could be headed to. He crept back to the woman's bedroom window just in time to see her enter the room, the same way as she had left out. The woman was still completely nude, when she re-entered the room. She went over to her dresser, grabbed a bottle of lotion, then went and sat on her bed.

Jerry watched as the woman put lotion on her body. The way that she was smoothly applying the lotion seemed erotic to Jerry and he found himself becoming aroused.

He was surprised when the woman spread her legs and put two fingers between them. He watched as the woman stroked herself with her fingers. He reached a full erection and had the urge to pull his penis out and masturbate right outside of her window. He fought the urge, because he thought if he did that it would be showing a sign of weakness. He promised himself that he would never be weak like James.

He watched the woman lay back on her bed and continues to masturbate. He could hear the soft moans that she was making through the thin glass. He also saw the look of pleasure that came over her face when she reached her orgasm. As he watched her climax, Jerry felt his penis start jerking and he realized that he was ejaculating inside his pants. Watching the erotic scene had caused him to ejaculate without even masturbating.

He cursed the woman for him not being able to keep from falling weak. He felt that the woman would have to slowly suffer for making him fall weak.

He watched the woman lay still on her bed for about two minutes. After she had regained her strength, she got up off the bed and went over to her dresser. She opened the top drawer, pulled out a long t-shirt and put it on. Afterwards she headed out of her bedroom.

He waited to see what light would come on next so that he could track her movements. After two minutes of waiting, he still did not see a light come on, so he crept around to the other side of the house. When he got there, he seen light coming out of a window and he approached it. When he got to it, he raised up in time to see her heading out of her kitchen, with what looked to be a sandwich in one hand and a bottle of water in the other.

Jerry seen a dim light illuminating from the window that was next to the kitchen and he went to it. He peaked into the window and seen that it was the living room. The woman had just turned the television on and was heading over to the couch, where she sat down with her legs folded under her.

Jerry knew that it was time to put his plan into motion. He went to the back of the house and went to the woman's back door and pulled the pouch out that held the metal strips inside of it. The pieces of metal were tools that were used to pick locks and that is just what Jerry proceeded to do.

Rebecca was sitting on her couch eating a late night snack and drinking some bottled water. She had the TV turned onto the late night news, but wasn't really watching it. She sat there thinking about how she was tired of spending lonely nights at home by herself. She was also thinking about how she was tired of having to play with herself until she reached an orgasm on those lonely nights.

She started to realize that if she kept waiting on James to take an interest in her that she was going to end up being a lonely old lady.

Something that she heard on the TV snapped her out of her thoughts. She heard the newscaster say that a woman had been murdered and how her body had been dismembered. What the newscaster was talking about sparked her attention and she sat up and tuned in to what he was saying.

"The police need help in identifying a man that is wanted in connection with the kidnapping and the murder of a Cleveland woman. If anyone can identify the man in these pictures, please call the Cleveland homicide department at the number appearing at the bottom of the screen.

Two pictures appeared on the TV screen. One gave a side view and the other gave frontal view of the man. When Rebecca seen the pictures of the man she dropped her half eaten bagel and her opened bottle of water to the floor. She did not need to see a clearer picture to recognize who the man was inside of it. She could not believe what the newscaster was implying what he had done. She sat for a few minutes replaying all of the weird behavior he had been displaying in the last month. She thought about how he had lied about knowing the nurse that was found dead on the side of the freeway.

It all started to make sense and she knew that it was her duty to call the police. She read the number off the bottom of the screen, and then quickly jumped up off the couch. She went over to the phone, picked it up and began dialing the number.

The phone rang four times before the answering service clicked on. Rebecca listened to the voice say, "You have reached homicide detective Mark Peterson. I'm not in right now so please leave your name and number, and I will get back with you soon as time permits it." Rebecca started to leave a message, "Detective Peterson this is Dr. Rebecca Rogers from the Metro …" that was as far as she got before she was grabbed from behind and a wet cloth was put over her nose. Before she could even realize what was going on she was unconscious.

Jerry quickly used the pieces of rope that he brought with him and bound both her hands and feet together. He pulled a roll of adhesive tape from his pocket and tore a piece off. He put the tape over her mouth then left out of her house.

He went across the street to the car, got in, then pulled it into her driveway. He pulled all the way to the back of the driveway, then reached over, opened the gloved compartment and hit the button that opened the trunk. Afterwards he got out of the car and went back into the house, where he lifted Rebecca's body and carried it out of the house. He placed her body into the trunk, closed it, then got into the car and pulled out of the driveway.

Jerry made sure that he stayed within the speed limit as he drove home. He did not want anything to go wrong on the drive home, because he had special plans for the woman that was in the trunk.

When he got home, he took the woman who was still unconscious out of the trunk and carried her into the house. He took her down to his office and laid her on one of his operating tables.

He decided that before he went any further, that he needed to replace James' keys and make sure that he was still peacefully sleeping. He went up to James' room, opened his door and found that he was still in a deep sleep. He put his keys back onto the nightstand, then left back out of the room and headed down to his operating room to perform surgery.

When he got back downstairs, he stripped the unconscious woman out of her clothes and strapped her down to the table. He did not put the head restraint on her, because he wanted her to be able to see the work that he had performed on her, when she woke up.

He went and got an IV that contained an anodyne drip and hooked her up to it. Next he went and retrieved the two trays that held his operating tools. He unraveled the cords on the tools that ran off electricity and plugged them into the electrical socket.

Once he had everything in place, he headed to his change room, where he put on his operating gear. He left out of the change room to begin a four step process. He intended to perform four surgeries on her over a four day period.

Jerry stepped into the cubicle, pulled the plastic curtain closed then began performing the first operation. It took him two and a half hours to complete the operation. He hummed his favorite song throughout the whole procedure.

When he was done, he stepped back to admire his work. A smile came to his face and he beamed with pride after seeing that the operation had been a success. He could not wait to see his patient's reaction, after she became awake and seen the work that he had performed on her.

Jerry thought that it was time for him to get some rest so that he would be fresh when he conducted the second operation. He took off his operating gear, stuffed all of it inside of a garbage bag, then went and took a long hot shower. Afterwards Jerry got into his bed and fell into a peaceful sleep.

27

The next morning when Peterson arrived at work he felt exhausted, because he had hardly gotten any sleep the night before. Something about the man in the picture kept nagging his brain. While his wife laid next to him sleeping peacefully, Peterson had sat up in the bed trying to figure out why the man seemed familiar to him. He sat up until the sun rose and it was time to get ready for work, but still hadn't found the answer. He had decided to take a cold shower before he headed to work to try and rejuvenate his body.

After the shower, he got dressed, then went downstairs and made himself a strong cup of straight black coffee.

While driving to work he found that he still felt sleepy and he opened the car window in order for the cool morning air to keep him alert. When he got to work Perkins was already there. She looked at him when he sat at his desk and knew that he had a sleepless night. She said to him, "You look a mess."

"I feel like one two."

"You just couldn't take my advice and get some rest?"

"It's not that I didn't try, it was just that some-thing about the man in that picture wouldn't let me rest. It seemed as if the pictures were talking to me. Telling me you know who I am."

"And did you figure out who he is?"

"I had no such luck." While they were talking the desk sergeant brought them both copies of the DNA results. Perkins had the DNA results from Miller. She looked at the envelope that held the results and dreaded opening them.

She finally got her nerves together and opened it. She wasn't too shocked when she found that Cody Miller's DNA did not match the DNA from the skin that was found under Weathers' finger nails and in her mouth. After she read the report her heart dropped to her stomach. She knew that she was going to have to re-evaluate her thought process as it related to her job.

She was about to show the report to Peterson but she seen that he had a report in each of his hands and was going from one to the other. She asked him, "So what are the results?"

"Well one confirms that the limbs and the head belong to Helen Morgan. This other one says that the torso belongs to a Maxine Hayes."

"Do you have any idea as to who that is?"

"No I don't, but let's find out." Peterson told her as he turned his computer on. He typed her name and social security number into his computer to run a check on her. He was surprised by what came back. The BCI check revealed that Maxine Hayes had numerous arrests for prostitution and soliciting. After seeing her arrest record, he whistled and Perkins looked at him and said, "Don't hold out, what did you find?"

"Well, it seems that Ms. Hayes was a prostitute that has quite a long record."

"That probably answers the question as to why no one has reported her missing." Perkins said to him.

Peterson looked at the information concerning her arrest and found that most of her arrests were made in the area of 40th and Detroit. He sat back in his chair thinking.

He knew that the heat was on and that he did not have long to close the case. He was trying to figure what his best move would be. He decided to check his answering machine to see if anybody had called to give an ID on the man in the picture.

He rewound his answering machine then pressed play and after a few seconds he heard a female voice say, "Detective Peterson, this is Dr. Rebecca Rogers from the Metro …" then the phone went silent. He sat there waiting to see if the woman's voice would come back on, but it never did.

He checked his answering machine to make sure that it wasn't malfunctioning and found that it was working perfectly.

He sat back in his chair and said out loud, "Now that's strange." Perkins who was sitting there still replaying the way she had treated Cody Miller in her head, heard his comment. She looked over to him and asked, "What's strange?"

"A woman called to leave a message and after stating her name the phone went dead." Peterson rewound the answering machine again, and afterwards he said to Perkins, "Listen to this," then he pressed play again. Together they listened to the message and when the phone went silent, they looked at each other.

"What do you think?" Peterson asked Perkins.

"I did not hear any click, indicating that the call was disconnected, play it one more time." she asked him. For the third time, Peterson rewound the message then let it play. They both sat quietly, listening for any clue that would indicate why the woman did not get to finish her message. They kept listening closely, after the woman's voice had stopped. They both found that they could hear what sounded like movement in the background. They could not tell exactly what was going on, but they did know that the phone did not hang up after the woman stopped talking.

"Do you think someone stopped her from finishing her message?" Peterson asked Perkins.

"I don't know, but whatever happened, it seems very strange."

"What's interesting is that she referred to herself as a doctor and if I'm not mistaken, I talked to a Dr. Rogers up at Metro when I went to re-interview Mary Weathers' co-workers."

"She mentioned the word Metro right before the phone went silent. She may have been referring to the Metropolitan hospital." Perkins said to him.

Peterson pulled out his notepad, and turned to the page that had the list of the people's names that he interviewed the day he visited the Metropolitan hospital.

When he got to the page, he ran his finger down it until it came to the name Dr. Rogers.

"Just as I figured, I did talk to someone by that name. I don't have a first name written down but I'm quite sure that it's her. I'm going to run her name just to make sure." Peterson said as he turned to his computer.

He punched in the name Rebecca Rogers and found that there were three women living in Cleveland who had that name. He also found that only one of them was a doctor. He wrote the woman's last known address down, then told Perkins, "Grab your jacket, we are about to pay Dr. Rogers a visit."

Perkins stood up, removed her jacket from the back of her chair, then together they headed out of the precinct.

On their way to their car Perkins asked him, "What's our first stop, her home or the hospital?"

"We are going to try her home first and if she is not there, then we are going to head up to the Metropolitan hospital. They got into their car and Peterson headed for the home of Dr. Rebecca Rogers.

28

Rebecca woke up from a drug induced coma. Although she had awakened, the anesthetic that was running into her body from the IV had her feeling like she was on cloud nine.

Even though her eyes were open, Rebecca did not believe that she was awake. Instead she thought that she was having a dream and the high voltage light that was positioned above her head only enhanced that perception.

She blinked her eyes several times, to find out if she were truly awake or dreaming. After blinking her eyes several times, they became adjusted to the bright light that hung above her and she realized that she wasn't dreaming.

She knew she was awake, but her head remained in a deep fog. She tried to concentrate and fought hard to clear her mind. After struggling to clear her mind, her senses only partially returned to her. The drug that was going in her arm from the IV, kept her heavily sedated.

Even with her senses only partially working, Rebecca knew that something was wrong with her. She got a feeling that a part of her was missing. She laid there feeling as though she was somehow incomplete.

She also got a feeling that she was bare. For some reason she felt as if she did not have a stitch of clothing on.

Rebecca knew that wherever she was, she was not supposed to be there. She tried to get up, so that she could leave, but found that her movements were restricted, because she was bound to whatever it was that she was lying on.

She decided to call for help in hopes that someone would hear her and come to her rescue. She tried to open her mouth and found that her mouth had been taped shut.

Not understanding what was going on, caused her to start crying inward and outwardly. Tears ran from the corners of her eyes, as her muffled sounds were held in by the tape that was covering her mouth.

She knew that she needed to clear her head to be able to figure out what was going on. She tried to turn her head and found that it was the only part of her body that was not restricted from moving.

She decided to shake her head from side to side in order to clear her mind, but she quickly found that doing that made her dizzy and disorientated. She lay still for a few minutes and when the dizziness subsided, she slowly turned her head to the right. What she saw when she turned her head disturbed her.

She saw two rolling carts sitting next to the table that she was strapped to. On one cart, she saw what looked to be surgical tools and on the other one she seen what looked to be carpenter tools. As she stared at them, she noticed what looked to be blood on both the surgical and the carpentry tools.

Her mind could not decipher exactly what it was that she was seeing. She gave up trying to figure it out and decided to turn the other way. She turned her head to the left and was more disturbed, when she saw the bottom half of a set of legs that had been severed at the knee. Rebecca could see blood dripping from the open flesh, where the legs had been severed. Her eyes went down to the ankle of the leg that was closes to her and she seen an ankle bracelet that was identical to hers. She wondered if it was her bracelet and if so, how it had gotten on the leg that was lying on that cart. She knew those were not her legs she was looking at, because she felt no pain.

She went back to concluding that she was in a dream, because she knew there was no way that her legs could be lying on the cart next to her.

She lifted her head off the table as far as she could get it, and then looked down towards her legs. She fainted when she seen that both of her legs had been removed right below the knees. All she seen before she passed out, were two nubs that were heavily wrapped in bandages. The bandages that were once white had turned bright red from the blood that was oozing from the wounds.

$$\lambda$$

Peterson and Parker pulled in front of Rebecca Parker's home and they both got out of the car and walked up onto her porch. Peterson knocked at the woman's door several time and got no response. He put his ear to the door and listened for a few seconds and it sounded to him as if the television was playing. Perkins asked him, "What do you hear?"

"It sounds like there is a TV playing." he replied. Peterson stepped away from the door and walked over to the living room window. He tried to find a place where he could peer inside of the window, but he found that the heavy drapes were completely closed.

He turned to Perkins and told her, "Let's go around back." Together they left the porch and walked to the back of the house. Back there, Peterson saw a two car garage that had a door with window panes in it. He walked over to one of the windows and peered inside. He saw a white BMW parked inside and he turned to Perkins and said, "If she is not home, she must have two cars, because there is a car sitting in there.

His investigative instincts kicked in and he walked to the back door, which led into the kitchen. He peered inside of the window, but did not see anything that would insinuate that there was someone inside. He put his hand on the doorknob and turned it and to his surprise the door was unlocked.

He stepped back from the door and drew his service revolver. Perkins had seen him draw his weapon, so she followed suit. Peterson looked back over his shoulder and told her, "Cover me," then he pushed, the door open and stepped inside. Perkins stepped in behind him, holding her gun at ready.

Once they were inside, Peterson with Perkins covering his back, followed the sound that he was sure was coming from a TV. The sound led them into the living room and upon entering, Peterson instantly seen the telephone receiver lying on the floor. He walked over to the couch and discovered a half-eaten bagel and a spilled bottle of water lying on the floor in front of the couch.

He turned to Perkins and indicating with his hand that he wanted to check the other rooms in the house. Moving quietly throughout the house, they searched every room inside the house and found no sign of Dr. Rebecca Roberts.

After they searched the whole house, Peterson said to Perkins, "From the looks of things, it seems that she may have met some foul play. We need to get CIU down here to dust for prints. Once they show up, we can head up to the hospital to see if anyone can shed some light on what may have happened to her."

The detectives sat in their car until the CIU team arrived on the scene then they headed up to the Metropolitan hospital.

29

James was at work, walking through the hospital making his rounds. He whistled as he walked through the halls, because he was feeling good. He felt refreshed after getting a full day's rest, prior to returning to work.

As he walked from room to room checking on his patients, he found that he did not have any worries on his mind. For some reason he was not even worrying about Jerry and the mess he had caused.

James also found that he felt mentally strong. He took that as a sign that he was gaining enough strength and would soon be strong enough to break away from Jerry for good. He realized that he was tired of Jerry considering him to be weak. While tending to his patients he had started to come to the realization that he was a grown man and that it was time for him to be his own man.

He even had thoughts of calling his ex-wife Melissa to see if they could reconcile. He thought about how happy he was those years that he had been married to her. Reflecting on how happy Melissa made him feel, made him yearn to have what they once had together back. He made the decision that as soon as he finished making his rounds and got back to his office he was going to call her. He entered into one of his patient's room and began tending to him.

λ

Peterson and Perkins arrived at the Metropolitan hospital and rode the elevator up to the sixth floor. When they got up there they approached the receptionist desk. Once there Peterson pulled out his wallet, flipped it open, then introduced himself.

"My name is detective Peterson and this is my partner detective Perkins. We are trying to locate Dr. Rebecca Rogers. Could you see if she is in please?"

"Sure," the receptionist said as she picked up the phone to page the doctor. She paged Dr. Rogers twice instructing her to report to the sixth floor receptionist desk.

After paging her the second time and getting no response, the receptionist paged the floor's supervisor. The supervisor arrived at the receptionist desk in less than two minutes.

Peterson introduced himself and Perkins to the supervisor and explained to her that they were looking for Dr. Rebecca Rogers. The supervisor picked up the phone and called to the hospital's assistant administrator to see if Dr. Rogers was scheduled to come in that day. The administrator answered his phone and the supervisor said to him, "Mr. Napoleon this is Ms. Hemmings from the sixth floor, could you check and see if Dr. Rebecca Rogers is scheduled to come in today?"

"Is there something wrong?"

"There are two detectives down here they say it is urgent that they speak to her."

"Detectives you say?"

"Yes sir,"

"Okay, hold on while I check." The supervisor was put on hold by the assistant administrator for about five minutes. When he came back on the line, he made sure that she was still on the line, "Ms. Hemmings are you there?"

"Yes, I'm here sir."

"I found that Dr. Rogers is indeed scheduled to come in today, but unfortunately she hasn't made it in yet. Ask the officers if there is anything that I can help them with?" The supervisor put her hand over the phone and said to Peterson, "She is due to come in today, but as of right now she hasn't made it in. The assistant administrator wants to know if there is anything that he can help you with."

Peterson thought for a minute then responded, "No, tell him that's alright." The supervisor relayed his message to the administrator then hung the phone up.

Peterson pulled a card out of his pocket and handed it to the supervisor. He told her, "If by chance Dr. Roberts does show up please hand her that card and advise her that I said it is important that I talk to her."

"I will relay the message detective."

"Thank you for your time and help." Peterson said to the supervisor before him and Perkins turned to head back to the elevator.

The elevator arrived and the detectives stepped onto it. The doors had yet to close before Peterson turned around and pressed which floor they wanted. As the doors began to shut a man wearing a doctor's coat came walking past. The man turned his face towards the closing elevator doors as he walked by. The man and Peterson made eye contact with each other and something inside of Peterson's brain clicked, "Son of a bitch!" he said out loud as he quickly tried to put his hand between the doors to stop them from closing. He wasn't fast enough and the elevator's doors closed and it started to descend.

Peterson became so anxious that he fumbled with the zipper on his jacket as he tried to get inside to retrieve something out of his inside jacket pocket. Perkins was lost by his actions and she asked him, "What did you see?"

"I saw the man that's in this picture!" he said as he finally got the picture out of his pocket and looked at it.

"What man are you talking about?" Perkins asked him.

"The doctor that just walked past the elevator as the doors were closing. Now I know why the man in the picture seemed so familiar to me. I just interviewed him the other day and he was adamant in trying to deny that he knew Mary Weathers, even though she had previously worked with him. Peterson passed Perkins the photo and she looked at it as he continued explaining things to her. "It was Dr. Rogers, who made him finally fess up that to the fact that he knew her. I have his name too." Peterson said as he reached back into his coat pocket and pulled out his notepad. He opened it to the page that had the names of the people that he had interviewed at the hospital on it. He found the name right below, Dr. Rogers' name.

Peterson read the name off the paper out loud, "Dr. James Mitchel." Perkins was still looking at the clean cut, timid looking man in the picture, when she asked Peterson, "Do you really think the man in this picture could be behind the murders?" Perkins asked him.

"Looks are deceiving, but let's look for facts." Peterson told her just as the elevator doors opened up on the first floor. They stepped out of the elevator and walked around to the first level of the parking garage. When they got to the entrance of the garage, Peterson stopped and started looking up at the rafters.

"What are you looking for?" Perkins asked him.

"I'm looking for cameras?"

"For what?"

"Well, the one on the third level does not cover all of the aisles, but there might be one on this level that covers the entrance and exit." Peterson said as he kept looking up.

Looking up into the rafters, he did not see what he was looking for, but when he brought his sights down and turned towards the security booth he said, "Bingo!" He saw that on top of the security booth there were two cameras pointing in the opposite directions. They were both pointed at a downward angle and they were positioned to see the faces of the drivers entering or exiting the parking garage.

Peterson turned to Perkins and said, "Come on!" Then he turned and headed out of the garage. He quickly walked back to the front of the hospital with Perkins right on his heel. He entered through the sliding doors and headed to the first floor receptionist desk.

The receptionist on duty was the same one who was on duty the last time he was there. She looked up and seen him approaching. When he got to her desk she said, "Peterson right?"

"Yeah, that's me."

"You're still looking for some footage huh?"

"Yes, but this time I know exactly what it is that I am looking for. I need to get back into the control room to look at some film."

"Okay, hold on, I will call security for you."

The receptionist made a call to the main control room and told them that there was a homicide detective at her desk and he wants to talk to somebody back there about viewing some video footage. She was told that the control room supervisor would be out shortly to speak with him.

After about three minutes a man dressed in regular clothes and had a two way radio on his hip approached the receptionist desk. He looked at Peterson and Perkins then introduced himself, "My name is Mike Jenkins and I am the control room supervisor. How can I help you?"

"I need to view the video footage that was captured by the cameras that sit on top of the control booth on the first level of the parking garage."

"If you don't mind me asking, why do you need to view the video?"

"Because it may help us identify a suspect that we believed was involved in a murder of a woman who worked here at this hospital."

"Do you know the date the footage was recorded?" asked the supervisor.

"It was taken last Thursday night at approximately 12:15am." The supervisor took the radio off of his hip and radioed to the control room.

He called for Ralph and he came over the radio, "Go ahead."

"Ralph, I'm on my way back with two detectives. They want to review video footage that was taken last Thursday around 12:15am. The footage is from the cameras that sit on top of the security booth on the first level of the parking garage. I need you to pull it up."

"Roger that?"

Peterson remembered that Ralph was the guy who helped him last time and he knew that Ralph would surely be able to help him.

The supervisor turned to the detectives and said, "Follow me." Both detectives followed him down the same hallway that Peterson had traveled down before. They got to the door that led in between the walls, entered it and then walked to the control room. When they got there the supervisor opened the door and escorted them in.

Soon as they entered, without being told, Peterson walked over to Ralph. He saw that Ralph had already brought the footage up. The date on the top of the screen read: 7-26-10 and the time on the bottom of the screen read: 12:05am.

Ralph turned to Peterson, who was standing behind him and said, "I figured I would go back a little further to make sure that we did not miss something."

"That's fine," Peterson replied as he watched the screen.

They patiently watched the video monitor until it read: 12:17am. At that time they saw a dark sedan pull up to the security booth to exit the garage. They watched the car come to a complete stop on the side of the security booth and the camera picked up a clear shot of the driver.

"Stop it right there!" Peterson shouted. Ralph quickly hit a button that froze the image in the video.

"Can you enlarge it?" Peterson asked him. Ralph hit another button and the image on the video became enlarged. Peterson pulled the picture out of his pocket and compared the image on it to the image that was on the video. He found that the image of the person on the video was identical to the image of the person that was in the picture.

"Son of a bitch!" he said then passed the photo to Perkins. Perkins looked at the picture then to the video monitor and she was surprised by what she saw. There was no doubt that it was the same man in both of the photos and the video footage.

Peterson got hyped and said to Ralph, "Ralph, I need you to do one more favor for me!"

"What is it?" Ralph asked him.

"I need you to print that image out?"

"No problem!" Ralph told him then hit a button. The supervisor went over to the printer and retrieved the picture after it was printed. He walked over and handed it to Peterson who then asked him, "Could you lead us back out front?" The supervisor led them back out front and the detectives headed straight for the bank of elevators.

Peterson pressed the button and the elevator doors instantly opened. They stepped inside of the elevator then Peterson pressed the sixth floor button.

They rode the elevator back up to the sixth floor and when they got there, they headed back to the receptionist desk. The receptionist was typing something on the keypad of her computer, when the detectives reached her. She felt their presence and looked up. Peterson told her, "I need the office number for Dr. James Mitchel." The receptionist typed something into her computer, then read the doctor's office number off to them, "It's room 615, which is right down the hall on the left."

"Thanks again," Peterson told her before him and Perkins headed down the hallway. They reached the door with the number 615 on it and Peterson knocked on the door. He knocked four times waiting five seconds in between each knock. He never got an answer, so he put his ear to the door and tried to listen.

He was trying to hear any sound that would indicate that someone was inside. He found that the thick mahogany wood, in which the door was made of, made it hard to hear anything through it. Peterson had been having luck with the doors he had been encountering. They all had been unlocked he decided to see if his luck was still good. He turned the doorknob and found that the door was locked.

He and Perkins went back to the receptionist desk for the third time.

They found that the receptionist was sitting facing the direction they were coming from, as if she was waiting for their return.

When they got there Peterson told the receptionist, "I need you to page Dr. Mitchel and ask that he report to your desk." The receptionist looked at Peterson strangely, but she honored his request. She paged Dr. Mitchel and they waited for him to arrive at the receptionist desk.

30

Little did they know, Dr. Mitchel had already gathered his things and left the hospital. All of the revelations that James had made only minutes before went out the window as soon as he locked eyes with the detective as he walked past the elevator. James was walking past the elevator, when something inside of him told him to turn to his left. He turned and locked eyes with the same detective that he had talked to a few days earlier.

The look that the detective had in his eyes made him nervous. He found that his hands were shaking badly as he quickly headed to his office. He stuck his hands inside of his pants pocket to prevent anyone from seeing how badly they were shaking.

He knew that he needed to warn Jerry that the heat was still on. He went to his office and did the same thing that he had done the day before. He called his boss and told him that he had to leave because of the same family emergency.

Afterwards he gathered his things and left his office, making sure that he locked it behind him. After waiting for over a half an hour and Dr. Mitchel not appearing, led Peterson to think that Dr. Mitchel knew they were onto him.

Peterson had the receptionist call the assistant administrator again to inquire as to the whereabouts of Dr. James Mitchel. The administrator informed the receptionist that not twenty minutes earlier Dr. Mitchel called and said he was leaving because of a family emergency. The receptionist explained what she had been told to Peterson.

Peterson shocked her when he reached out and took the phone out of her hand. He put the receiver up to his ear and told the administrator, "This is homicide detective Mark Peterson and I am investigating the murders of Mary Weathers and Helen Morgan. Dr. James Mitchel is a suspect in both cases and it is urgent that I get into his office. I also will be needing his home address and any other information that may lead to his possible whereabouts.

The administrator was baffled by the accusations the detective was lodging against Dr. Mitchel. The administrator knew that the hospital and the community looked at Dr. Mitchel as a highly respected doctor. He did not know how the detective had reached his assumption, but the administrator refused to jeopardize his career by withholding information.

He decided he was going to accommodate the detective's request and just hope that it proved that he was wrong. He told Peterson, "I will be there shortly with the key to his office and the information that you have requested." Peterson thanked him and then hung the phone up.

The administrator pulled up Dr. Mitchel's home address on his computer and wrote it on a piece of paper. He then picked up the phone and called the person that was head of security for the hospital. He told him to meet him at the receptionist desk on the sixth floor immediately. Once he completed the call, he headed out of his office.

The administrator arrived at the receptionist desk a second before his security personnel. He saw both Peterson and Perkins as he approached the desk. When he reached them he introduced himself, "My name is John Napoleon and I am the assistant administrator here at the hospital." Not wanting to waste any time Peterson said to him, "We can make the proper introductions as we walk to Dr. Mitchel's office. Did you bring the key?"

"Joe here is the head of security for the hospital and he has the key." Peterson took off heading back to Dr. Mitchel's office and the administrator tried to keep up with him. He wanted a better understanding of what was going on. As they briskly walked down the corridor, he asked Peterson, "Detective can you give me more in depth details as to what is going on?"

"Dr. Mitchel is the suspect in the murder of Mary Weathers."

"There has to be a mistake, Dr. Mitchel is regarded highly at this hospital as well as in the community."

"All that is fine and dandy, but it doesn't take away from the fact that he is the suspect in not one but two murder cases."

They reached Dr. Mitchel's door and the security guard looked towards the administrator who shook his head, giving him the go ahead to unlock the door. The security guard took the keys off of his hip and found the master key that opened most of the office doors. He unlocked the door and Peterson told him and the administrator to step back. He drew his service revolver and so did Perkins. He turned the knob on the door and pushed the door opened. He stepped inside with Perkins right behind him. He searched the room for a sign of Dr. Mitchel but found none.

He stepped back out of the office and asked the administrator, "Did you bring his home address?"

"Oh yes, I almost forgot." he said as he pulled the piece of paper out of his pocket that had the doctor's home address on it. He handed the paper to Peterson, who took off down the hall with Perkins at his side.

They rode the elevator to the bottom floor then headed out to their car. When they got into it, he handed the paper to Perkins and told her, "Call in to get a search and arrest warrant for James Mitchel and have back up meet us at his address. Perkins used her phone to call the DA's office about obtaining a warrant. She advised the DA to send someone from his office with the warrant. She read the address off to him then hung up. Next she picked up the mic for the car's radio and radioed in to dispatch and asked that backup be sent to 14311 Brook Park Road. The dispatcher let her know that back up was on the way. Peterson turned the car's sirens on as he drove as fast as he could on his way to the doctor's house.

31

Rebecca had regained consciousness and she laid there praying. She was asking God what it was that she had done to deserve to be in the situation that she was in. She laid on the table replaying her life in her mind. She was trying to remember anything she could have done in the past that would justify what she was going through. She couldn't think of anything that she could have done that made her worthy of having both her legs removed. She wanted to see the face of the person that had kidnapped her and severed her legs. She wanted to ask them the question why.

She found that she wasn't going to have to wait much longer, when she heard the sound of a lock turning.

Rebecca laid there with her eyes opened listening to the footsteps that were descending the stairs. She listened as the footsteps got closer and closer, then all of a sudden, they started heading away from her. She knew that the person was still near, because she heard him humming what sounded like a song.

About five minutes later she heard the footsteps coming back towards her. The footsteps stopped for a second, and then she heard a curtain being pulled opened. The footsteps were right upon her, when she raised her head and seen the person approaching her. She could not believe who she was looking at. She became so confused by who she saw, that for a minute she felt disorientated and thought she was going to pass out.

The man seen her looking at him and stopped humming the song. He acted as if he did not see her as he plugged the cords of the electrical tools into the sockets. Rebecca looked at the man as he walked around the table and moved the table that had her legs on it. He pushed it out of the cubicle and brought in another cart that was empty and placed it next to the table. Rebecca knew then that he intended to do her more harm. She started crying again and tears began to run down her cheeks like a flowing river.

Jerry walked around the table and picked up the power saw. He was getting ready to complete phase two of his patient's operation. He positioned himself over her then turned on the saw. Before he brought it down to remove her right arm he looked in her eyes. The tears that ran from her did something to him. His conscience started to bother him and he started to feel that what he was about to do wasn't right.

For a minute his face showed a temporary sign of compassion. He pulled the tape from her mouth and said to her, "I'm so sorry Rebecca."

Rebecca felt that she had a chance of talking him out of doing her anymore harm. She began to beg him, "James, please don't hurt me anymore! Why are you doing this to me?" She looked into his face with pleading eyes and watched how his face started transforming through many different expressions. The last expression that came upon his face was that of pure rage. The man said to her with the mask of rage, "You deserve to die, you are weak and you are making James weak."

Rebecca could not understand why James was referring to himself in third person.

"I don't understand James!" she said in between her sobs.

"I'm not James, he is a weakling. After I kill you, James will no longer exist?"

"What have you done to James?"

"I had to bury him, so that I could protect him without interference. You will soon be buried too!" he said to Rebecca as he turned on the power saw. He raised it and all of a sudden, he heard a big boom coming from upstairs then he heard what sounded like numerous footsteps coming inside of the house. Jerry said to his self, "They have come for her. I have to finish the operation quickly." He brought the saw down where Rebecca's arm connected to her shoulder and started cutting through her flesh. Even though Rebecca felt no pain because of the drugs running through the IV, seeing her arm being severed made her scream. Her scream let authorities know exactly where she was.

Jerry cut all the way through her right arm and the only reason it did not fall to the ground was because of the strap that had it secured to the table. Rebecca passed out from going into shock after seeing her arm get cut off.

Jerry heard the footsteps approaching the basements door and hurried around to the other side of the table. He raised the saw to bring it down to remove her left arm, but him being in a rush had caused him to pull the cord out of the electrical socket. He quickly ran back around the table and plugged the cord back in and as he was on his way back around the table, the cubicle's curtain was snatched open and at least ten cops were standing there with their weapons pointed at him. Peterson who was in front of the pack told him, "Dr. Mitchel put that saw down. You are under arrest for murder."

Jerry knew that there was no way out. He knew that everything had finally come to an end. He figured that the only thing left for him to do, was to save James from having to spend the rest of his life in prison.

He put his finger on the switch that turned on the saw and went at the group of policemen. He only made it one step before he was cut down by their line of fire. He was hit over twenty seven times before he fell to the floor. James and Jerry Mitchel both died right there on their basement floor.

The police did not too much worry about the body that was lying on the floor, they were trying to save the woman who had nearly been totally dismembered. Peterson thought that it was a miracle that she was still breathing. He knew that she had to be a strong woman to endure all that she went through.

The news cameras showed up right after the ambulance that came to transport the woman to the hospital. When Peterson stepped out of the house, the reporters flooded him with questions. He and Perkins stopped and the reporters formed a circle around them. Peterson told them that, "I will answer a few questions then me and my partner have to head back to our precinct."

The reporters fought for position, trying to get their mics in front of his face. A reporter from channel eight news asked him, "Detective what led you to believe that a prominent doctor, such as Dr. Mitchel could be involved in such heinous crimes?"

"Good investigative police tactics led us to believe that Dr. Mitchel was involved in the murders of Helen Morgan and Mary Weathers." A reporter from channel three news quickly jumped in with a question, "Detective, what about the torso that was recovered with the missing limbs, do you attribute that death to Dr. Mitchel also?"

"My guess is that Dr. Mitchel was involved in that murder also, but we have to wait for forensic evidence to be tested in order for us to be one hundred percent sure. I'll take one last question, and then I have to be going."

A reporter from channel five news asked him, "Detective have the authorities figured out Dr. Mitchel's motives for committing those heinous acts?"

"That is a question that we will probably never know, but one thing we do know is, because of where he is at right now he will never be able to kill again." With that, he and Perkins walked to their car, got in and headed back to the precinct.

λ

While Peterson drove he and Perkins were both trapped inside their own thoughts. Sitting in the passenger's seat, Perkins laid her head on the headrest. She closed her eyes as she reflected on her past personal experiences and how she had let them affect her decision making on the job.

Sitting there with her eyes closed, she decided that she was going to take a long needed vacation then afterwards she was going to seek out counseling. She also made the decision that she was going to give Cody Miller a face to face apology.

She concluded that the case she just worked proved to her that it's not always the most obvious, who be guilty. She learned that sometimes it be the ones who you least expect, that be guilty. She hoped that after attending counseling, she would go back to work with a new perspective on life and the way she did her job.

Peterson was trapped in his own thoughts. He did not know whether he should feel good or bad. He thought to himself, "Yeah, I have taken a cold blooded killer off the streets, but how many people did he kill, before I finally got him?" He thought about the torso that was missing body parts. He realized that as long as he worked in homicide he would always stay feeling conflicted. He took in the fact that he solved a murder case that day, but he knew he would be faced with solving another one the next day. As he drove to the precinct he wondered what the next murder case would entail.

He concluded that it did not matter whatever it was he would be ready for it.

www.ingramcontent.com/pod-product-compliance
Lightning Source LLC
Chambersburg PA
CBHW072102170626
46813CB00004B/1427